LORD HALE'S MONSTER

STEVE HIGGS

VINCI
BOOKS

Vinci Books

vinci-books.com

Published by Vinci Books Ltd in 2025

1

A CIP catalogue record for this book is available from the British Library.
Paperback ISBN: 9781036708634

The EU GPSR authorised representative is Logos Europe, 9 rue Nicolas Poussion, 17000 La Rochelle, France contact@logoseurope.eu

By Steve Higgs

Blue Moon Investigations

Paranormal Nonsense

The Phantom of Barker Mill

Amanda Harper Paranormal Detective

The Klowns of Kent

Dead Pirates of Cawsand

In the Doodoo with Voodoo

The Witches of East Malling

Crop Circles, Cows and Crazy Aliens

Whispers in the Rigging

Paws of the Yeti

Under a Blue Moon

Night Work

Lord Hale's Monster

Herne Bay Howlers

Undead Incorporated

The Ghoul of Christmas Past

The Sandman

Jailhouse Golem

Sparks in the Darkness

Shadow in the Mine

Ghost Writer

Monsters Everywhere

This book is dedicated to all the fans of the Blue Moon series who harassed me mercilessly until I wrote this instalment. It was so much fun to craft the latest adventure, please pester me again.
Sorry it took so long.

Hale Manor

'This place sure is spooky.' Tempest was sitting in the passenger seat of my Mini and was staring out the windscreen to the enormous manor house to our front. Rain lashed down against the car, another early winter storm and it was the type of day when you would be glad to just stay indoors.

We didn't have that option though. We had committed to attend a birthday party event at a manor house a few miles from where we lived and worked in Rochester. The rather eccentric Lord Hale was turning eighty and believed he would be visited by an ancestral curse this very night. The story, which was a great one to tell around the campfire, was that every second generation of Hale died on his eightieth birthday when an unspeakable monster visited the house. The generations that avoided the horror of this fate, died at a ripe old age as had been the case with the current Lord Hale's father.

Tonight, with a few friends, Tempest's parents and a

sense of adventure, we were having dinner at a party in Lord Hale's honour and seeing if we could usher him through the weekend still alive. That was the challenge it seemed, and he offered the firm a substantial sum just for turning up. Whether we still got paid if Lord Hale perished was yet to be discussed.

Lightning sheeted across the sky, blinding me for a second with its brilliance. 'We are going to get wet,' I observed. The manor house was hundreds of years old, and parking was going to be outside, not in a convenient underground garage that a modern building might have. The dash from the car to the great house was going to be through deep puddles and even if we could run through it quickly, we were going to have to come back for Tempest's parents to help them with their bags.

It was a formal dinner tonight in ball gowns and dinner jackets. That made it extra fun because Tempest looked great in a suit, and I was certain he would look even better in a black bow tie. My name's Amanda Harper, by the way. I used to be a cop, but I met Tempest a while back and took a job working for him as a paranormal detective. Somehow we got close, I guess that's one of those things that happens in a close working environment and mutual respect led to mutual attraction and suddenly we seem to be a couple.

Not that I am picking out what flowers I want in my bridal bouquet or anything, it's just some casual fun, but I like him, and it would be nice for things to work out for once.

I wasn't entirely sure about having his parents along with us for the weekend though. I liked his dad; he was funny and a lot like Tempest in a slightly cheekier way. However, his mother is an acquired taste. She always seemed to say exactly whatever was in her head and looked at me as if Tempest's only interest in me should be my ovaries.

Another flash of lightning lit the manor house. Tempest was right; it was spooky. It looked like the house from an episode of Scooby-Doo. All it needed was some bats flying around the turrets. Even the trees around the castle looked nasty. Devoid of leaves now that autumn had denuded them, their twisted black branches looked like evil fingers clawing at the sky.

Looking up at the tower now, I noticed something and pointed. 'Hey, Tempest. The light is on in that tower.'

He craned his neck to see. 'It certainly is.'

'Huh.' There wasn't much else to say about it. It looked odd, a single lit window way up at the top of the tallest tower, but maybe it had been turned on for something weeks ago and they forgot to turn it off and hadn't noticed. Or maybe they put it on for effect with the dinner tonight and the storm. Just as I took my eyes back to the road, something passed in front of the window. I glanced at the road, to check I was still on course and not drifting and looked back up. 'I saw something.'

Tempest craned his neck again. 'In the tower?'

'Yeah, I think someone's up there.' We both continued to stare for a few seconds but whatever I thought I saw didn't come back. 'Maybe I imagined it.'

Tempest shrugged and settled back into his seat.

'Hey, girl,' said Patience from the back seat. 'I don't like the look of this place. I think we should turn around and go home.'

I glanced at her in the rear-view mirror. Her eyes were bugging out as she scooched down to look out the front of the car. 'I thought you were looking forward to seeing Big Ben.'

'I was. I am. Maybe he and I should go somewhere else though. You two crazy people can stay here at the death castle, and I'll take Big Ben to the Travelodge.'

'Big Ben doesn't know you're coming remember. It's going to be a big fancy dinner plus drinks and entertainment.' I turned to look at Tempest. 'Is there entertainment?'

He pursed his lips and frowned. 'The invitation didn't say. It said we would be fed and have full use of all the facilities at the manor house. It went on to name some of the things we could do but I doubt anyone is going to bother with the tennis courts this weekend.'

'I'm sure there will be some entertainment,' I assured my nervous friend on the backseat. The single road leading to Hale House took us far off the beaten path and out onto the Hoo Peninsula where the backdrop to the house was nothing but open sky. Half a mile behind the house the countryside ended and fell into the sea. There was nothing out here for miles around.

'Hey, girl!' Patience was sounding worried again. This time she was staring at her phone. 'I just lost all signal to my phone.' She was swinging the phone from one side of my car to the other and holding it up to the sunroof in a bid to get the signal back. 'Oh, my goodness. I have no phone signal!'

Next to me, Tempest slid his phone out of a pocket and checked it. 'No signal,' he concluded. 'I guess we are too far out from populated areas.'

'You mean we're in a dead zone,' gibbered Patience on the back seat.

I frowned at her. 'You're being dramatic. We can manage without our phone signal for a few hours. Besides, I

4

bet they have a signal at the house. It will be hardwired in so once we are there your phone will work just fine.'

'We'll find out soon enough,' said Tempest as he put his phone away. He was right; we were nearly there now. The only manmade thing in sight in any direction was the manor house. There were no cows or sheep in fields, no pylons running across the countryside; we were truly miles from anywhere but somehow still less than sixty minutes from the office.

The manor house's dominant position and the view it had over the countryside meant that no one could easily sneak up on it. We were expected of course, but as we reached the end of the long drive and swung the cars around in front of the house, one of a pair of very large oak doors opened and a man came out with an umbrella above his head. He had several more umbrellas hooked over his right arm.

I noticed that Tempest was squinting out of the windows. 'Do you see that all the windows have shutters on them?'

I looked. 'Yes. What of it?'

He pursed his lips and he frowned. 'Nothing. They just look out of place on an ancient house, and they look so solid, like they might be designed to keep things in not out.'

One thing to note about Tempest was that he could be a little paranoid. Admittedly, it saved his life every now and then, but I doubted our host had anything sinister planned for us. 'Is that Frank's car?' I asked, pointing to a dirty brown Rover 400.

Tempest nodded. 'It sure is. I wonder if he came with his date or is meeting him here?' I rolled my eyes at Tempest's question. Frank didn't have a date. He was attending with another man though, a man that specialised in the paranormal and one who was known to us both: Dr Lyndon Parrish.

A couple of months back Dr Parrish set up a rival firm and began poaching customers from Blue Moon. It didn't last long, and Dr Parrish reconsidered his business plan after he ended up in hospital and we ended up with his abandoned and rather plush office. It worked out well for us in the end.

'Do you know who else is attending?' I asked as I pulled on the parking brake.

Tempest shook his head. 'The guest list is secret. I only know about Dr Parrish through Frank, and I only know Frank is coming because I asked if he wanted to come with us and he had to admit he already had an invite. All the crazy people are coming to town.'

'Mm-hmm,' said Patience, 'and we seem to be leading the march.'

The rain continued to beat down as we gathered our belongings. Mercifully, my ballgown was inside a plastic cover, as was Tempest's dinner jacket. Patience hadn't been so forward thinking though so her taffeta number with sequins was going to get wet and be ruined if we couldn't cover it. In the end we decided to come back for it with my plastic cover once my dress was safely inside.

A knock on my window made me jump. It was the man with the umbrellas. I powered the window down just a touch so I could hear him speak as he was bending down to the window. The man looked to be ninety years old and frail as a dry twig. He was dressed in tails and black bow tie: the quintessential butler. He might have been with the house since it was built.

Rain bounced off the edge of the window to splash my

face. 'I have umbrellas to protect you from the rain,' the man said. His voice came out like he was chewing gravel.

'Wow!' said Patience. 'That's a zombie. Amanda, this house is the spookiest place on earth, the butler is a zombie, and we are all going to die. You need to get this car back in gear and get the heck out of here.'

Ignoring her, I glanced at Tempest. 'Ready?'

He grabbed his door handle. 'Not much point waiting.' We bailed out simultaneously, my overly dramatic friend on the backseat still swearing that we would die if we went inside as I ducked under the partial protection of the butler's umbrella. Tempest ran around the car to join me, and we both took umbrellas from the man's offered arm.

Tempest's mum was in the car next to us and staring out the window. We motioned that we would come back and ran with our umbrellas, bags, and suit carriers to the wide-open doors at the front of the house. Then we ran back to get Patience, though I had to more or less force her from the car and then we went back for his parents.

'It's a bit wet,' said his dad as we sploshed through the puddles to the house. We were in though and not that damp really. Behind us, the large oak door swung shut with a terrible creaking groan. The butler pushing it with both hands to make it move. Just inside were two more men, one younger than the butler by about sixty years which made him about Tempest's age. He was also about Tempest's size which stood him in stark contrast to the other man who was closer to Big Ben's height but bulky rather than lean and muscular. He was in his late forties and might have had grey hair showing though if his natural hair colour wasn't white blonde. His eyebrows matched. The more attractive man's hair was dark brown, and both wore it very close-cropped.

They were collecting bags and loading them onto a trolley. They wore a similar uniform to the butler.

As Patience came in, she caught sight of the younger man bending over to pick up a heavy bag and murmured, 'Hubba, hubba. Mmm hmmm. If Big Ben doesn't show, I get first dibs on him, okay?'

'If you would like to follow me, please,' croaked the butler to save me from having to respond to Patience. 'I am Travis, Lord Hale's butler,' he announced. 'I started here as third footman in nineteen thirty-nine and have been the head of the staff for forty-seven years.'

I exchanged a glance with Tempest. The man had been working here for eighty years. Assuming his age wasn't in single figures when he started, he had to be getting close to a hundred years old now.

'How many staff are there now?' asked Tempest taking an interest.

'Just five, sir. Mrs Holloway the cook, Miss Polonowski the cleaner, young Matthew and Alexander, the footmen,' he indicated the men pushing the trolley of bags, 'and myself.'

Patience flared her eyes. 'There's got to be a hundred rooms in this house. How do they manage?' she asked the question on a hushed breath but if the butler heard it, he didn't bother to answer.

Tempest stopped though and was rummaging in his bag. 'Travis, my dear fellow, the invitation states that there is a spa and gymnasium and a butler in every suite.'

'Oh, no, sir,' the old man seemed tickled at the suggestion. 'I think someone was having a little joke with you.' If that was the case, then I didn't see what was funny about it.

From the large entrance lobby, we followed Travis along a wide passageway. It had bare floorboards, polished to a high shine and covered here and there with expensive-looking rugs. Rooms appeared in pairs on either side, one left one right, with large doors that were closed to mask what might be inside. The passageway opened out ahead of us. As it did, we came into a grand hub with four spokes going off it and twin staircases sweeping left and right to the next floor.

At the top of the stairs was a man in an elegant suit.

Lord Hale

SATURDAY, DECEMBER 10TH 1724HRS

The old man spread his arms wide in welcome and cracked a broad smile. 'This must be the Tempest Michaels' party. Welcome all of you to my humble home.' He began descending the stairs. 'Thank you for arriving in good time.'

Tempest went forward to shake the man's hand as he reached the bottom of the stairs. 'Tempest Michaels. Thank you for the invitation.'

'Goodness, no, thank you, young man. I fear your skills may be tested to the very limit this night. Are there more to join you yet, I count only five of the eight in your party.'

'Yes, the other three will be along shortly, other commitments delayed their departure. May I please introduce the rest of my party?' Tempest then turned to face his father, introducing him first, followed by everyone in the group one at a time. Lord Hale shook hands warmly with each of us.

When he got to Patience, she said, 'What's with the Wi-Fi in this place? I can't get a signal on my phone.'

The old man chortled. 'I'm terribly sorry, my dear. There's no internet signal here. They offered to hook me up, but I refused. Blasted infernal modern technology. We're better off without it if you ask me.'

Patience stared at her lifeless phone and started to hyperventilate. Then she stuck out a hand which flailed as it tried to grab me for support. 'No phone. Amanda, there's no phone. I think I need to lie down.'

Lord Hale eyed her quizzically. 'Is your friend alright?' he asked.

I cocked an eyebrow at him. 'Compared to what?' When I saw I had confused him further, I added, 'She'll be fine. She's just a little dramatic. Where are our rooms please?'

'Ah, yes. Travis will escort you to your accommodation where you can relax and change for dinner. Some of the other guests have congregated in the billiards room for pre-dinner drinks. Please join us there when you are ready. Dinner will be served sharply at eight.'

Lord Hale inclined his head with a smile and walked away across the room to disappear around a corner.

'This way please, gentle folks,' requested Travis, trying to scoop bags so he could carry them. Tempest and I quickly retrieved them from him; he moved slowly enough without being weighed down with extra items.

Like everyone else, I couldn't help glancing about the grand house. It was enormous and the central hub we were now in stretched all the way up to a glass ceiling high above. I counted four stories above us and wondered how many houses in the country, or even the world, were bigger than this one.

Every wall was adorned with carved wood panels, oil paintings and tapestries. The floor was hard stone but most of it was covered by ornate rugs and there were candles everywhere though none of them were lit.

I expected to be led up the stairs to our rooms, but Travis walked toward a wall ahead of us instead. It was only when I was about to ask where he was taking us that I spotted the elevator. It was perfectly camouflaged in the wood panelling so only the button's gentle glow at waist height gave it away. I might have walked by hundreds of times and never noticed it was there.

A press of a button and the doors slid open to reveal a shiny steel box inside. Travis led us inside but instead of pressing a button to take the elevator to its next destination, he entered a four-digit code on a panel. 'You're all on the first floor. You can access the house using the stairs.'

'Why not the elevator?' asked Tempest.

Travis turned slowly to make eye contact, his body creaking from the effort. 'I'm afraid, sir, that it accesses private areas of the house. This is why we have a security code for its operation.'

I don't think Travis's answer did much for Tempest's Spidey-sense. He posed another question. 'Why does every window have a set of shutters on it?'

This time Travis kept his eyes front as he answered so we couldn't see the emotion on his face or read his facial cues. 'We are close to the coast and very exposed here, sir. Storms can be violent.' That seemed to be all the explanation he felt was necessary.

Tempest pressed on though. 'How long does it take to shut them all?'

'It's an automated system, sir. The house has a control room from which the window shutters can be locked.'

'You mean closed,' Tempest confirmed. Travis didn't reply and Tempest shot me his suspicious eyes.

When Travis pressed the button marked with a number one, I noted that the house had a basement and a sub-basement assuming that was what B1 and B2 meant. 'What's in the basements?' I asked.

Travis didn't answer, and it felt deliberate that he used the elevator's arrival on the first floor to mask his lack of response. The doors opened and he shuffled off along a passageway with us following.

As we passed a window, Tempest caught sight of the front of the grounds outside. 'Look,' he said, pointing. 'Caterer's vans. I guess that's how one cook can manage to feed all the guests.' As we looked down, Big Ben's unmistakable enormous black utility vehicle swung into a parking spot next to a van with a slew of gravel as he pulled on his handbrake.

Travis had shuffled down the corridor ahead of us, but Tempest wasn't one for asking permission ever. He reached up to open the window, and despite the rain he leaned out to shout at his friend.

Big Ben looked up at his name being called. 'Alright, bender,' Big Ben's voice echoed back; he was always so loud and gregarious.

'Yes, hello, Ben,' replied Tempest. 'We're on the first floor. Where are the newlyweds?'

'They broke down and had to call for a mechanic. Actually, they broke down, couldn't get a signal and I had to drive back two miles until I got a signal and then call a mechanic. I offered to bring Alice here with me rather than leave her stuck in the cold and wet, but Jagjit made like he didn't trust me with his wife.'

'I can't think why,' I said at normal volume so Big Ben wouldn't hear. Tempest just grinned at me.

'Anyway, they won't stop touching each other and saying nice things to each other. It was making me feel a bit sick. I need to distract myself, send me some pictures of Amanda getting changed. That should do it.'

'Yes, Ben, Amanda is standing next to me and can hear you,' Tempest sighed.

I put a finger to my lips to keep Patience quiet and then stepped up to the window and called out, 'Hi, Ben.'

'Hey, everyone,' Big Ben called back unconcerned that he had just asked my boyfriend to send him naked pictures of me. Tempest's mother tutted. She did not approve of Tempest's large friend and I could understand why. Big Ben was a walking mountain of testosterone. At six feet seven inches tall he had a face that could have made him a Hollywood film star and a muscular body that would have made him the greatest warrior in ancient Rome. 'The rain just got even harder,' Big Ben shouted up to us. 'I'll catch up shortly.' Then he was gone, and silence returned as Tempest pulled the window shut once more.

'Big Ben's here,' said Tempest unnecessarily.

Travis had stopped walking and was waiting for us to catch up. When we reached him, he announced that we had reached the first of our rooms. They were all the same and all huge. We took a look inside the first one as Tempest's parents filed in. It had to be sixty feet in each direction and contained a four-poster bed. I shot Patience a look and got a grin in return.

The next room was for Tempest and me, but I dropped my bags at the door and went with Patience to her room. 'How are you going to surprise him?' I asked her as she threw her dress on the bed.

'I haven't decided yet, but that boy had better be pleased to see me or there's gonna be trouble.' I laughed at her. Big Ben and Patience were very much alike in their approach to relationships; neither one wanted one, but they were both very happy to fool around. Patience climbed onto the bed. 'Maybe I should…'

I held up my hand to silence her. 'I don't want to know. Just have fun okay. It's more than two hours until dinner, but try not to be late, eh?'

'Two hours, huh?' Patience thought about that. 'I might have time to get the cuffs out.'

I put my hands over my ears and made a, 'lalalala,' sound to drown out anything else she might say. Back in my room, Tempest had unpacked his dinner jacket and my dress and had them both hung up to let any creases fall out. He had also shucked his shirt and was looking quite delicious.

I needed to do my hair and makeup and shave my legs but… well, we had two hours.

Guest List

SATURDAY, DECEMBER 10TH 1947HRS

I sent Patience a text message saying I would meet her downstairs and hoped things had gone according to plan with Big Ben, then realised she wouldn't get it only when it failed to send. I had a tiny clutch bag that would carry a phone and a lipstick and nothing else unless it was very small, but there seemed little point in carrying my phone if I couldn't use it. I threw it in at the last moment anyway and stood up ready to go.

'Shall we?' asked Tempest. Like a typical man, getting ready had taken him about five minutes, three of which was trying to tie his bow tie. His short hair dried in minutes and needed only the gentlest persuasion to form a suitable style. For the last half an hour, while I had scrubbed and tidied and crimped and worked my way through the two dozen stages I required for a night in a ball gown, he sat quietly reading a book.

Finally ready to go, he offered me his arm so I could hook a hand into his elbow, then we locked up and knocked for his parents. There was no answer from them. 'I guess they went down already,' he said. 'Let's go find them.'

It was easy to track them down thankfully. Though I had been concerned we might roam the enormous house aimlessly looking for the other guests, we were drawn by noise and light. Most of the passageways were not lit, so we followed the ones that were, the sound of conversation growing louder ahead of us. When we found an open door and heard a roar of laughter, we knew we had found the right place. Inside, someone was telling a funny tale.

The person, it turned out, was Tempest's dad. He had the room's attention as he regaled them with a story. Tempest's mum had a grumpy expression on her face and the look of someone that wanted her husband to stop talking. He was clearly winding up for the big finish when we walked in. '…and then he said, I bet you can get twice that for it in Bangkok!'

I had no idea what story he had told but everyone in the room was laughing. Everyone except Tempest's mum, that is, probably because she had heard the story a dozen or more times before. I spotted Frank just as he spotted us, but other than Tempest's parents, I didn't recognise anyone else in the room.

Frank was crossing the room to greet us; he seemed in fine mood, a broad grin on his face. 'Hello, Amanda. Good evening, Tempest.' He shook Tempest's hand and kissed my cheek.

'Where's Dr Parrish?' Tempest asked.

'He just stepped out. He'll be back soon.'

'Tempest Michaels,' a woman's voice called across the room.

Our heads swung in her direction just as a petite African

woman detached herself from a small group to come our way. Tempest clearly knew her from somewhere.

They embraced briefly, a quick air-kiss, then he turned to me. 'This is Gina. I met her in Cornwall in October when I was trying to work out what the pirates were.'

'Pleased to meet you,' I said as she shook my hand. 'Are you connected with the paranormal?'

Tempest answered for her. 'Gina hails from the scientific discovery end of the spectrum.'

'I have some of my colleagues with me actually.' She turned to welcome three men who were coming across the room to join her. All three had beards and were in their fifties or sixties. 'I would like to introduce Professors Wise-man, Larkin and Pope.'

More hands were shaken as Tempest and I met the three men and then Dr Lyndon Parrish rejoined the room. 'Dr Parrish,' Tempest acknowledged as the two men locked eyes. Their relationship was adversarial or would be if Tempest considered Dr Parrish to be worth competing against.

'Mr Michaels,' replied Dr Parrish with a brief nod of his head. He made sure to accentuate the word mister to differentiate himself as a doctor. I knew Tempest thought the man was an idiot and doubted anything would change his mind tonight. I never met him when his rival firm was in operation. It opened just as I was leaving the police but was gone so quickly that our paths never crossed. He and Tempest sat in distinctly different camps on the belief system.

The room was filled with an eclectic mix of people; some looked to be by themselves where others were in groups like Gina and her professors. One man looked like a magician, another like a spy or a detective from a fifty's noir movie. Scanning around, I next spotted a very attractive woman in her mid-forties sat in one corner ignoring everyone as she sipped a Bloody Mary while watching the dynamics of the room like a hawk scanning for prey. I asked who she was, and though Tempest didn't know, Frank leaned in to tell me her name was Lady Emily Pinkerton and that she was a vampire. Tempest shot me an amused smile and inside my head I joked that it probably wasn't a Bloody Mary she was drinking after all.

I continued to scan the room. As someone moved, I spotted a short person. I didn't want to label him as a dwarf, but he had a bushy beard and long hair tied into braids that flowed over his shoulders and he was a shade over four feet tall. All he needed was some armour and he could walk onto a *Lord of the Rings* filmset ready to go. Then there were five women, dressed in earthy colours and wearing necklaces of braided flowers and lots of silver. If I had to guess, I was going to say they were witches of some kind. It was quite the guest list and they were all here for the same reason; to save Lord Hale from the monster he believed was going to kill him this weekend.

Of Lord Hale, the eccentric, enigmatic host, there was no sign, until just before eight o'clock when Travis reappeared in the bar with a small gong. He hit it with a soft hammer. 'Ladies and gentlemen, your host, Lord Hale.' A polite smattering of applause rippled around the room even as Lord Hale waved for it to stop.

'I want to thank you all for coming. In a few short hours, the clock will strike midnight, and it will be my eightieth birthday. I do not expect to survive the day and have known for most of my life that it would be the day on which I would die. The legend of my family is one that stretches back centuries, but I do not know what event, what treachery or evil was perpetrated to have caused such a curse to befall my family. That is why I have asked you all here tonight. When the monster strikes, when it comes for me, it is my hope that the greatest minds in the paranormal community will be able to prevent the beast from dragging me to my doom. My hope is that between you, you will be able to isolate the monster or determine what motivates it so that the curse can be undone.'

As if on cue, lighting flashed across the window behind him. Then the gong sounded again, and, like a ghoul, Travis appeared from a dark shadow by the doorway. 'Dinner is served, sir.'

'Patience and Big Ben aren't here yet. Neither are Jagjit and Alice,' I hissed at Tempest. He just shrugged. I guess he was right in that there wasn't much we could do about it. Mercifully, Big Ben and Patience appeared as we got to the door, Big Ben still tying his bow tie and looking flustered for a change.

Patience winked at me. She had been having a good time then. She snuck in next to me as the guests all filed after Lord Hale and Travis. 'Girl, I need some food. I am starving. I worked up such an appetite.'

'How did he take it?'

'Girl, listen to you getting all personal about my sex life. Well, don't you worry, sugar, because I got all kinds of details to share with you.'

'No, I mean, how did he take the surprise that you were here. Tempest basically lied to him about the whole thing.' I had no desire to hear what Patience got up to with Big Ben. I suspected it would scare me.

'Well, you know Big Ben; he comes around pretty quick when there's some action to be had. I was on the bed waiting for him, so when he came in, I let him know what was on offer and that was that. He just kinda shrugged and said he was gonna kill Tempest later.'

'Are you feeling better about being here now?' I asked as we filed into the dining hall. It was a huge, vaulted room with a long table running down the entire length of it. Thirty seats were set up, fifteen along each side with one at the very end for Lord Hale. There was some shuffling around for people to find their seats as each place had a little name card next to it. Our first course, which appeared to be a cold ham hock salad was already served and there were platters of fresh bread and bottles of wine on the table.

'That looks a bit small,' Patience commented, eyeing the delicate portion on her plate. 'Do you think there'll be some chicken to follow? I could eat me some fried chicken right now.' I doubted the cook was planning to serve fried chicken. I also wondered what decorum we would need to follow tonight. Was Lord Hale about to say grace? Would there be staff to serve food? We knew there were caterers here, but were they doubling as wait staff?

Just as everyone lined up behind their chairs and gentlemen moved to pull out chairs for the ladies, all the lights went out. Patience shrieked right next to me, which made me jump, my hands grabbing the chair so I had something steady to anchor myself. The room was still lit by a row of candles down the centre of the table but the flickering light from them did little to keep back the gloom. The room had no windows, but it did have a fireplace and from it, a low moan began to emanate.

The fireplace was directly behind Lord Hale. I saw the old man turn to face the sound as it grew in volume. 'You are early!' he cried. The moaning noise was unnerving; it sounded like a voice.

'Tempest, what's happening?' shouted his mother. His parents were on the opposite side of the table, his father with an arm around his wife to comfort her but I could see they were just as disturbed by the turn of events as I was.

Next to me Patience was going nuts. 'Arrrrgh! There's a monster coming. I knew I should have stayed home. This is God punishing me for enjoying the company of men. Tomorrow, if I get out of this, I swear I am going to church and I'm gonna pray. And that money I was gonna use to get a wax. I'm gonna put that money in the collection box.'

Then the table began to rattle. Only a little at first, the gentle sound of the crockery and cutlery knocking together, but then with more vigour and a wine bottle fell over, Patience catching it before it could spill and taking a deep swig to calm her nerves. It was like being in an earthquake, I imagined, but the floor wasn't shaking, just the table.

To the other side of me, Tempest was calm, but he looked unhappy. I had no idea what was going on and I couldn't imagine he did either. However, he refused to believe in anything he couldn't see or touch so I wasn't sure what he would make of this. I held onto my chair; it was solid and stable which was good because I had to admit I was getting a little freaked out now. Then the moan from the fireplace, which had sounded like an onrushing wind, reached a deafening crescendo and burst forth carrying soot and dirt with it. The candles all went out instantly and Lord Hale cried out in terror.

The room was thrown into utter blackness but only for a second as people touched their phones and little pools of light appeared, followed by bright swathes of light as people activated their torch apps.

I managed to fumble mine out from the little clutch bag too and that was when I saw a sight that would stay with me for the rest of my life. Looking down the table as cries of fear tore from the throats of men and women alike, I saw that a huge monster had a man in its grip. I was rooted to the spot, but the dinner guests at that end of the table were coming my way, all of them trying to get away from the creature.

Like a bear crossed with a spider it had a large body and walked upright but its forelimbs were spindly and long. On its head, eyes glowed a deep orange like traffic lights fitted with a low wattage bulb and blue light spilled from its mouth like warm breath on a cold morning. It was grotesque.

Then, as it lifted the man into the air by his throat, it spoke. 'All will perish here tonight.' The sound of its voice was like no sound I had ever heard before. A rasping noise like metal being filed mixed with a lion's deep roar.

Everyone in the room was frozen in fright or trying to get away from it. With a final snarl, which elicited a fresh round of gasps and squeals, the monster turned and ran, reached the wall behind it and clambered up to disappear through a hole in the ceiling.

Torch light tracked it as it fled and then there was nothing but silence.

Ham Hock Terrine

The silence stretched for a couple of seconds and then everyone started moving and talking at once. The range of responses was diverse to say the least. Patience ran screaming for the door. I heard a thump as she hit it and it failed to open. I swung my torch to find her sprawled on the floor. Tempest's mother was crossing herself and saying some kind of prayer while his father held her. Toward the head of the table, Gina and the three professors were talking fast in animated terms; the four of them had formed a huddle but they looked excited more than anything.

Lord Hale appeared stunned by the event. His face ashen, and a hand on the table to steady himself, others soon saw him and came to his aid. 'Yes, yes, thank you,' I heard him reply as they settled him into a seat.

But a whoop of delight caught everyone's attention. It came from Frank and he had a huge grin plastered across his face. 'Deny that, Tempest Michaels!' he laughed. 'Tell me that was a man in a costume!'

Patience interrupted before Tempest could respond.

'Hey, stupid white people! We're locked in! Will someone please join me in panicking.' Then she went back to kicking and thumping the door.

Tempest made a tutting noise with his mouth; it was the sound he made when he was thinking. I turned my attention to Big Ben. 'Ben, do you have a cigarette lighter with you?' In response, a flame flicked into life next to me. 'Let's relight these candles, shall we?'

As light from the candle in front of me cast fresh shadows, I turned off the torch on my phone to preserve the battery and sat down. Tempest saw me, flashed a smile of agreement and took his seat too.

Over my shoulder, I called out to get Patience's attention. 'Patience, won't you join us? Our starters look delicious.' All along the table, the guests began sitting. 'I'm hungry,' I announced. 'I'm not sure what just happened but adding hunger to the confusion will not help.' Then I picked up my knife and fork, selected a bread roll from the platter and started eating. There was a faint trace of soot from the chimney but not enough to stop me from eating. It gave me something to do while my adrenalin settled. As I swallowed the first bite, I asked, 'Lord Hale, who was it that the monster took, please? I didn't get the chance to meet him before dinner.'

From the head of the table, Lord Hale, still looking bewildered, said, 'His name was Mortimer Sebastian Crouch. He was a paranormal investigator much like you and Mr Michaels. I had to talk him into coming and now I feel responsible for his death.'

'Are you sure he is dead?' Tempest asked, deliberately challenging the concept.

I had a better question though, 'Why did he take Mr Crouch and not you, Lord Hale?'

Lord Hale looked down at his plate, shaking his head from side to side as if having an argument with himself. 'Perhaps because my birthday is not until tomorrow? He said, "All will perish here tonight." I think he means to pick us off one at a time. We must work together to defeat it or capture it and escape this place.'

Dr Lyndon Parrish was the first to offer an opinion on the monster itself. 'What I believe we just saw was a demon. It manifested physically, so we can quickly conclude that it is not a ghost or spectre. Apparitions such as memories of the dead cannot take physical form. It was clearly not a lycanthrope, skinwalker or shifter of any other kind and did not resemble any creature that I have ever read about. Demons, however, can take any form they choose.'

From the far end of the table, Gina spoke up, 'Our field of expertise is paranormal psychology. My colleagues and I are somewhat lost with physical supernatural beings, but whatever that was, it was not a ghost.'

The man next to her chipped in. 'Our equipment might have been able to measure energy readings from it, but alas, it isn't yet set up. It was our plan for after dinner.'

I felt the chair move next to me as Patience returned to the table. 'Really?' she asked. 'We are going to sit and have some nice dinner now? That guy just got eaten by a monster, why is no one else freaking out?' The answer to her question was that I was indeed freaking out. I was doing my best to keep a lid on it though because it would do me no good to panic.

Tempest cleared his mouth with some water and spoke, 'As the eternal sceptic in the room, I will say that I cannot yet explain what we saw.' Frank whooped again. 'However, once I have eaten this lovely ham hock terrine, I plan to find my way out of this room and then start looking for the missing man. Something is going on and I would like to get to the bottom of it.'

Sitting opposite him, his mother poured herself a generous glass of red wine and downed half of it. 'That thing said we would all perish tonight. I think I would like to go home now. Perhaps, Tempest, you would be so kind as to locate the nearest exit for us before you spend too much time working out what that thing was.'

'Of course, Mother.'

'It should be possible to summon the creature and trap it,' said Dr Parrish between bites. 'We need to know its name to do that and a few other vital pieces of information, but it might be possible to draw it into a demon trap if it returns for any of us.'

Frank rummaged in a pocket. 'I have a pocket watch.'

'What's that for,' I asked.

Dr Parrish answered, 'To hold the demon, we need to freeze time. We can do that symbolically by stopping the hands of the clock provided the pocket watch is inside the circle when we close it.'

Tempest laughed at me. 'You really should learn to not ask questions.' He was right, it just encouraged their craziness. 'This ham is lovely,' he commented as he scraped together the last few morsels on his plate. 'I think though, that we should start looking for a way out. Don't you agree?'

I did, and so did most of the others, though the scientists had gone into a huddle and were arguing about something. I left them to get on with it as I pushed back my chair and stood up. I planned to do something productive now. I had no idea what that might be, but I wasn't in the mood to be trapped anywhere so whatever I was going to do, the intended enterprise was escape.

Just to my left, beyond Big Ben, another man was also

getting to his feet. I hadn't paid him much attention until now, but the flamboyant swish of his arms caught not only my attention, but that of almost every set of eyes in the room.

'I think,' he started, 'that perhaps it is time for me to announce myself.' He was the man I mentally labelled as a magician when I first saw him in the bar. In his late fifties, his grey hair was shoulder length and pulled into a ponytail behind his head, his grey beard was close-cropped but also full, so it covered his entire face and he wore round glasses with a wire rim. 'My name is Caratacus Soulfull. I am a representative of the British senior council of wizards. Like the rest of you, I am here at Lord Hale's request.'

'Of course you are, dear chap,' said Big Ben, smiling down at the smaller man. 'Can you do the one with the rabbit? Hold on. No, how about the one where you make a saucy assistant appear? That would be good.' When the wizard ignored him, Big Ben persisted. 'You must have a saucy assistant. Even the rubbish magicians on television have a saucy assistant.'

'I am not a magician!' the wizard roared, and with that he took several paces back and began to move his hands in circles.

'This should be good,' whispered Tempest who had come to stand close to my back, the material of his jacket brushing against the exposed skin of my shoulder.

Dim light appeared to emanate from the man's fingers as they twirled. Then I began to feel the air moving and the strange sense of static electricity in the air. 'I shall conjure a spell to detect our exit from this room,' Caratacus announced, his focus and gaze absorbed by what his hands were doing.

It was an impressive display of convincing nonsense, if

that was all it was. However, in the darkness of the room, I couldn't tell that the man wasn't actually weaving a spell. A ball of light now began to grow in his right hand. Sparkling and fizzing as if alive, his right hand stayed still as his left hand continued to dance around it, then with a whispered command I could not understand he pushed his right hand down to the floor and the ball of light vanished into the wooden floorboards.

Fascinated, I watched, transfixed just like everyone else in the room as the spell started moving across the floor. It appeared to have a life of its own, the sparkling light now mostly hidden as if inside the wooden floorboards, so it appeared only as pinpricks visible through small knot holes or bore holes from long-dead woodworms.

As if insulted by the display, Tempest swung his torch to the floor and got onto his hands and knees to follow the light as it moved away.

Across the table, Frank cackled again. 'I told you, Tempest. I told you there was more to this universe than you could explain.'

The wizard's spell hit the wall and split off, heading both left and right as it tracked along the wood panels. It vanished behind oil paintings and tapestries but always emerged again, the faint sparkles seemingly inside the wall as the spell continued onwards.

'What's it doing?' asked Patience, her voice hushed and quiet the way mine might have been if I had spoken.

Caratacus was watching the light just as intently, or perhaps even more so than the rest of us, but swung his attention to Patience now. With pride in his voice, he boasted, 'It is finding our way out of this room. It is a seeking spell of my own design; one I have been perfecting over many years.'

'How does it work?' asked Tempest with no sense of sarcasm or irony in his voice.

The wizard shook his head. 'The occult arts are not for mortals to know.'

'You're immortal then, are you?' asked Big Ben. 'Can we test that? I've always wanted to meet someone that thought they couldn't die.'

'I am demi-mortal,' Caratacus explained. 'I live a significantly longer time than a normal man. I am currently in my one-hundred and fifty-first year, but I am not immortal as you suggest and can die just like anyone else.'

Big Ben just sniggered. 'Well, I wouldn't want to cater your birthday party. Imagine all those candles.'

The spell had now tracked all the way to the grand fireplace at the end of the room where it stopped. Where it had split into two parts, the other half tracked a longer route to arrive at the same place. Tempest continued to track it along the wall, knocking on the wall, presumably to find a hollow point or work out how the effect was being produced.

'There is an exit behind the fireplace,' announced the wizard, snapping his fingers. The sparkling lights extinguished to leave the wizard smiling at us with a triumphant expression. 'All we need do now is work out how to access it.'

'Really?' asked Tempest's father. 'A secret exit behind a fireplace? Isn't that a little clichéd? What next? Trap doors?'

'Don't wish too hard,' I murmured to myself as I started following the wizard, and pretty much everyone else, toward the fireplace.

Patience caught hold of my arm. 'Amanda, is this a wind up?' she asked. I could hear the hope in her voice.

I offered her a wry smile. 'Patience, I wish I had the

resources to organise this kind of wind up for you. I have no idea what is going on, but I do intend to get out of here. Whether there is a way out through the fireplace or not, remains to be seen, but there are enough of us here to force our way out if it comes to it.'

That was a good point actually. Patience had hammered on the doors and announced them locked, but no one else had tried to open them since. I changed my direction, bumping into Big Ben in the dark but gave him a shove. 'I need your muscles, big boy. Come along.'

'Now we're talking,' he replied, swinging around to follow me. 'Nothing like a near-death experience and the threat of a horrible end to make the girls want some action.'

I rolled my eyes and tutted. 'Ben, you are such a dickhead. I want to see why this door won't open. We came through it not long ago and it looked like an ordinary door to me. Now it won't open? There's something screwy going on.'

I reached the door with Patience and Big Ben on my shoulder. We weren't alone though; another man had detached himself from the crowd. It was the dwarf. 'Shouldn't we all be helping to get out through the fireplace?' he asked.

'Why?' I asked in reply without turning away from the door. 'This is the door we came in through. Why don't we go back out through that?'

'I thought your friend said it was locked?' he replied.

'It is,' said Patience.

'And the wizard believes there is a way out for us over there,' the dwarf added.

I got on my hands and knees, being careful to sweep my ballgown out of the way so I didn't kneel on it, then used the light from my phone to look underneath the door. Scanning all the way along, I looked for a bolt or some other kind of physical barrier that would prevent the door from opening. The gap under the door was small, maybe three or four millimetres but it was enough to be certain that there was nothing visibly preventing the door from opening.

I stood up again. 'Ben, can you look at the top? See if there is something physical to stop the door from opening?'

He replied and took my phone when I offered it. He had to stand on his tiptoes to look but he found nothing there either.

'It will be magnetic,' came Tempest's voice from behind me.

The dwarf turned to face him. 'I think we should all help with the search to find our way out through the fire-place, don't you? You seem to be the sceptic of the group? You saw the wizard's spell, are you able to deny what you saw?'

'Yeah, Tempest,' said Frank, clearly enjoying himself. 'What about the wizard's spell?'

Tempest chuckled to himself. 'Frank, I want you to really enjoy these moments, because when I show you the man orchestrating all these neat little tricks, you will be eating humble pie for a long time.' He turned to his dad, someone who I knew had some experience as an electrical engineer. 'What do you think, Dad? If it's magnetic we just need to cut the power to it, right?'

'Or short it out.' His dad turned and looked around the room. Then spotted the bottle of wine in his wife's hand. 'Mary, give me that a moment, won't you?'

He reached for the bottle, but she snatched it out of his reach. 'Get your own. This'uns mine.'

Muttering, his dad walked to the table where he found a jug of water instead. 'Water will work better anyway.'

More of the crowd from the fireplace had moved down to see what we were doing. I could hear the wizard and another man trying to get everyone to come back. 'There will be a switch or a lever somewhere, we just need to search for it,' said Caratacus, trying to encourage everyone to help out.

Lord Hale's voice also echoed out of the dark. 'This is a very old house. Priest holes, secret passages and the like were not uncommon when it was built. I should not be surprised to find an exit behind the fireplace.' His voice sounded hopeful to me, like he was hoping we would abandon what we were doing and try the wizard's daft idea.

'Or it might be a secret incantation,' Dr Parrish suggested, joining in. 'I bet there are clues in the room somewhere. I would put in clues to open a secret door if I was building one.'

'Yes,' agreed Lord Hale. 'Well done, that man. Now we are thinking.'

Tempest's dad stepped up to the door with the jug of water. 'We need to get it flowing over the switch and down to earth in order to create a short. That might be difficult, or even impossible from this side as we need to convince the water to flow over the top of the door and down the other side and we need to guess where the magnetic lock is.'

'It will be in the middle?' I suggested.

'Most likely yes,' Tempest's dad agreed. Then he handed the jug to Big Ben. 'You've got the legs, big fella.'

Big Ben took the jug and stepped up to the door. 'Hold on,' I called as I fetched a place mat from the table. 'Use this to guide the water over the top of the door.'

With Tempest holding the mat and Big Ben pouring the water, we all held our breath to see if our assumptions were right. About half the water went over Tempest, not that he seemed to care, but we could all see it pooling on the floor and that enough of it had flowed over the door and down the other side.

Nothing happened.

There was no hopeful sparking noise or the pop of a solenoid opening. Pursing his lips, Big Ben put the jug down, then made everyone jump as he kicked the door with all his might. The mighty thump echoed around the room and he swore, lighting the room with some choice expletives.

'You okay?' Tempest asked him.

'I hurt my foot,' Big Ben admitted. 'That's a solid oak door.'

Tempest's father clapped him on the shoulder. 'It was a good try. They'll be another way out though.'

Big Ben picked up a chair to examine. 'We ought to be able to make a lever out of something.'

'Or we could just go out through the fireplace,' suggested the dwarf yet again, as if we were all being ridiculous.

'They don't appear to have found a way out yet,' I pointed out. 'I wish them luck, but I think we should all be trying to find alternatives.'

Gina, the petite African woman Tempest knew, appeared from the shadows. An unwelcome voice at the back of my head whispered that she and Tempest might know each other a little better than I might like. There was no sense in my jealousy or need for it, but unwarranted or not, it raised its annoying head.

'How can we be of help?' she asked. I think the question was aimed more at Tempest than it was at me, but she was looking at me when she said it. 'It seems we are all in this together. I guess we all need to pull our weight.'

Big Ben swung into view, creating a shadow just by existing. 'Hello, I'm Benjamin Winters. You can call me Big Ben.'

Georgine gave him a curious look. 'Why?'

Big Ben placed his right thumb in his mouth and mimed blowing into it as he expanded his impressively wide chest and stood up straight to show that he had been stooping. 'Because I am big, and my name is Ben. I will be happy to show you just how big I am when we find a more appropriate time.' Her jaw dropped at his forwardness.

Tempest, being used to his friend's behaviour, ignored it. 'Since the door does not wish to yield willingly, I suggest we either find a way to force it as Ben suggested, or we start trying the wall panels to see if any are hollow and do the same with the floorboards.'

'Did you hear something?' Patience asked.

Everyone around me paused to listen.

A second passed. Then another. Just as I opened my mouth to ask her what she thought she might have heard, I heard it too. The faint sound of music, a reedy woman's voice singing something in a high trill. It was coming through the wall or floor or through a vent somewhere and was accompanied by instruments – so a record being played.

'Find the source,' I murmured, not wanting to speak so loud that I drowned out the faint noise. With something productive to do finally, many of those who had until now just observed, started to fan out.

Ears were being pointed at floorboards and wall panels as the group spread out.

'It's coming from behind the fireplace,' called the wizard, a tone of victory in his voice. 'There will be a way out through here, you can bet on it.'

Our search led us to the conclusion that he was right about the source of the music at least. It was strongest over by the fireplace. Standing inside the enormous hearth, which was deep enough and wide enough to fit ten people in comfortably, I turned my face up to the chimney. Something was amiss. I turned on my torch again but the beam from it vanished into the darkness before it found a surface above me. I couldn't see light coming down nor hear the storm outside wailing over the chimneys.

'We should be able to hear the storm,' I said aloud.

Tempest came to stand under the chimney with me. 'Yes. It ought to be creating a venturi effect and be drawing air out. There ought to be an updraft here.'

'Why isn't it lit anyway?' asked his mother, also joining us. 'It's December and this is a huge house. It should be colder in here than it is.' She made a valid point. There was no visible heating anywhere in sight and the fireplace, designed to supply the huge room with heat, wasn't lit in the middle of a winter storm.

'The house uses pipes dug deep into the soil to circulate warmth back into the house. The pipes run though the wall cavities and under the floorboards, the water in them continually circulating,' explained Lord Hale. 'The fireplaces are grand but are unnecessary now.'

Tempest wasn't buying it. 'Nothing here adds up,' he growled, typically annoyed by the unexplained phenomenon; he didn't like not knowing what was going on.

His thoughts were interrupted by the sound of the dwarf dragging a chair across the room. He was coming directly towards us as we stood in the fireplace. When he saw us looking at him, he kept coming a few more feet then stopped and started to climb onto the chair. 'I think I might like to have a weapon with me,' he said as he reached his hands above his head.

I had to step out of the fireplace to see what he was after, but there, above his head was a heavy-looking and ancient battle-axe. Even standing on the chair he was too short to reach it.

Big Ben, without comment for once, reached one hand up and grasped it for him. It gave him some resistance though. 'It's stuck on something,' he said as he too stood on the chair to see what was holding it in place. With a huff of exertion, he tore the axe free, but something clicked as he did, and the world started moving.

Tempest and his mother were still standing inside the fireplace and had to jump clear as it began to move. The sound of stone dragging across stone filled the air and dust filtered down from the ancient fireplace as the back wall moved slowly away from us.

The wizard gave a small air pump with his right fist and a, 'Yes!' of triumph as a passageway came into sight behind the fireplace.

'Oh, jolly good!' exclaimed Lord Hale. 'Perhaps may see the night through, after all. If only I knew what drove the beast in its desire to kill me, maybe then we could stop it. Something in my family's history has to have caused it.'

'Yes, Lord Hale,' the wizard agreed. 'Stopping the monster would be our best solution. Perhaps we should explore your family history as we find our way out. At least it seems my spell was accurate.' Caratacus came around me, as I was one of the nearest to the fireplace and looked ready to lead us out. As he peered into the passageway beyond, he turned to face us. 'Shall we?'

'Well, would you believe it,' uttered Tempest's dad,

staring at the new passageway. 'If that isn't the darndest thing I ever saw.'

I felt like hesitating but where else could we go? There appeared to be no other way out of the room, so though I could offer no explanation for the wizard's magic show, or for the appearance of a secret passage behind a fireplace, I also couldn't see any point in remaining where we were. I heard Tempest tut to himself, an indication that he was mulling over the same choices I perceived.

'I vote we see where it leads,' I offered.

Tempest tapped his chin a few times as he thought. Then he glanced back at Big Ben and his father. 'I vote we prop this thing open with the table or something in case it leads nowhere.'

'Good thinking, kid,' his dad agreed.

'I think we will stay here,' said Gina, appearing out of the dark again. 'It seems safe enough here...'

'Are you crazy, girl?' asked Patience, interrupting the smaller woman. 'Did you not see the enormous monster, beast thing? What if he comes back? You want to stay here with the beard brigade that's your business, but good luck killing it with algebra.'

'Algebra?' Gina echoed, sounding mystified.

Patience cocked a hip. 'Yeah, or calculus or some other clever sciency stuff. You eggheads love to baffle people, well, don't expect that to work on a demon. That's all I'm saying.' Then she hooked an arm through Big Ben's and clung onto him. 'I ain't going more than about six inches from this hunk of man. He can protect me.'

'Um,' said Big Ben.

The wizard was already in the passageway, Frank and the dwarf with the axe and several others following him. Lord Hale's voice echoed back along the narrow tunnel, 'I think we should stay together. It will be much safer if we do. No telling what might visit that room yet.' He clearly wasn't waiting for us, the light from his group was already fading as they made their way along the hidden passage.

Tempest grabbed a piece of table, Big Ben shucking Patience's arm to grab the other end. 'Let's just secure our return in case it becomes necessary, eh?'

They turned the enormous oak table over, grunting and straining from the effort even as more of us joined in. With it upside down they jammed it into the hole the retreating fireplace created in such a way that if the fireplace wished to close the gap again it would have to crush the solid looking table to do it.

It wasn't going to happen.

I turned back to Gina and the group of remainers. There were about ten of them, which included her three bearded colleagues and the witches. The flower women had been largely silent thus far and hadn't yet introduced themselves. 'We're going,' I told them. 'Good luck here. If we find a way out, we'll either circle back or send for help.'

Tempest's parents had already gone down the passageway, following Big Ben and Patience and a few others. Tempest was waiting for me, standing on the upturned table in the fireplace. Moving to join him and wondering what we would find when we arrived at the source of the music, I got only a foot or so into the tunnel when I heard a noise coming from the room we just left.

I could best describe it as a wheezing breath but that fails to capture the despair and anguish the sound managed to portray. My feet froze, Tempest's too as we both came to a halt.

Shocked gasps and cries of fear from the dining room drew us back through the fireplace just in time to see an apparition form in the room. An ethereal, ghostly shape began to take shape, hovering in the air above the table and I could feel cold air blowing against my face when a mouth formed, and it began to speak.

'Be gone from this place.' It uttered in a dread voice. I found the voice to be familiar and as the mist continued to take form, I realised what I was looking at was a giant head that closely resembled Lord Hale. Was it supposed to be one of his ancestors perhaps?

Behind me Patience screamed, the sound cut off suddenly when Big Ben clamped his hand over her mouth. Gina, her colleagues and the other group of women were all backing away toward the fireplace now as if driven there by the ghost.

'Be gone,' Lord Hale's ancestor said again. 'While you still can.'

'Why?' The question came from Tempest. He was staring up at the giant ghostly head and looked like he wanted to punch it. 'Why are you playing this giant charade? What are you to gain from it?'

'Fool,' the head replied. 'Go now and escape this place or share my fate.'

Then, the cold air that had been a gentle breeze became a strong wind, the icy temperature nipping at my skin as if I were being bombarded by ice crystals, and I felt myself being pushed backwards by it.

Gina, the professors, and the others who elected to remain in the dining room all changed their minds and ran through the fireplace and down the passage behind it. Only Tempest and I remained, and I really wanted to go. Not just because this thing was giving me the creeps, which it was, but also because I was getting really cold from the icy air.

Lord Hale's face then transformed from benign older

gentleman into horrific tortured version of the same. Tendrils of mist in the form of snakes sprang from his eyes and the mouth dropped open as the head screamed. Then it charged, moving from its position halfway down the room to blast towards the pair of us. My feet took an involuntary step backward but Tempest, my hand in his, held firm. The apparition washed over us and vanished.

Tempest said, 'Hmmm. I'm not sure what to make of that.'

'What do you mean?'

He wheeled around and started after everyone else, keeping my hand in his he led me over the upturned table and down the passage. The light from other people's phones provided enough light for us to see them by. Once we were walking down the passage, he said, 'I can't work out how any of this is being done. I'm not prepared to assume that was a real ghostly head, but I couldn't see a light source from which it was projected. Whoever is doing it has gone to some trouble. I just don't know why.'

With hurried steps we caught up to those who had gone ahead. The sound of music grew louder as we continued along the narrow passage. It wound around several corners but then we reached a jam of people.

'What's going on?' I asked, raising my voice so I would be heard.

Mirror

The passageway stopped ahead of us where it reached a door. The wizard, at the front, had elected to wait before opening it, probably trepidatious about what might be on the other side. With the press of people ahead of us, Tempest and I were stuck at the back, but I had no reason to feel that we should go first. I was as confused as everyone else about what was going on and content to follow the crowd until there was something I could do to help our situation.

Before we could question what we were waiting for, Caratacus pushed the door open. It creaked like it was a prop from a horror movie but swung open to reveal the space on the other side was just as dark as the one we had come from.

'Power must be out everywhere,' Big Ben commented as we filed into the new room. The room was filled with children's toys. Old ones from a century or more ago. There was a rocking horse, its brightly painted livery still visible in the dim light, and a doll's house that was as tall as me plus several large china dolls, their hair teased into curling locks. In one corner was a record player although it was a really old one with a handle on the side to wind it up. I thought the correct term for it might be gramophone, but I wasn't sure. Someone had to have wound it recently though, so there was someone else creeping around ahead of us.

'This is the spookiest toy room I have ever seen,' said Patience. 'Someone tell me there is another door.'

There was. It was locked but the key was in it. The dwarf, still carrying the axe in one hand, was undoing the lock when Dr Parrish rested a hand on his arm.

'Stop,' he demanded, his tone insistent. Then he held up a candle and lit it and we all watched as the orange flame sparked and fizzed and gave off a blue tinge.

'Sulphur,' hissed Frank.

'Dear lord, what now?' I asked, getting bored with all the weirdness.

The wizard flourished his arms again, waving them high in the air before bringing them to rest either side of his shoulders as if he had just loaded them. 'There is something beyond the portal.' His clear voice cut through the hush.

'Portal?' echoed Big Ben with a snigger. 'Most people just call them doors.'

'On my count, open it,' the wizard commanded. The dwarf, who was nearest, took it that the command was aimed at him and readied his hand on the door. Frank and Dr Parrish backed away as the wizard once again called light into his hands, odd nonsensical words filling the air as he chanted a new spell.

'I need to get a look at the light in his hands,' said Tempest, letting go of my hand to cross the room. He didn't get there in time though.

The wizard called, 'Now,' and the dwarf yanked the

door open. What happened next stunned everyone, including Tempest.

On the other side of the door was a mirror, the wizard's face suddenly visible as it stared back into the room. But then the wizard was sucked into it, becoming one with his own image as he vanished inside the mirror. The balls of light conjured into his hands were instantly extinguished and then he turned to stare back at us, his shocked face staring back out of the mirror which was no longer reflecting our faces back at us, but showing us the wizard trapped on the other side of the glass.

We could see him shouting but the sound wasn't getting to us. Gasps and choked sounds of surprise echoed around the room. I, too, was stunned by what I could see, my brain unable to supply an explanation.

Tempest took a step forward and just as he did, the wizard conjured another ball of light into his right hand and threw it at the surface of the mirror he was trapped inside.

The glass shattered, fragments falling in tiny shards to the floor to reveal a new passageway beyond and a set of stairs leading down.

Of the wizard, there was no sign.

Reflection

Lord Hale, who had been nearest the wizard when the mirror smashed, jumped back in fear, 'Great Scott!'

'Where'd he go?' wailed Patience, while next to me, Tempest's mum crossed herself for the umpteenth time. Tempest just sighed.

Dr Parrish called Frank over to the smashed pieces of mirror with a hand gesture. 'What do you make of it, Frank? It appeared to be a soul trap.'

'Exactly what I was thinking,' Frank replied. 'I've never heard of one being used in this hemisphere though. Have you?'

Looking disconcerted, Dr Parrish shook his head. 'No. Not before tonight.'

'What's a soul trap?' asked Professor Wiseman, leaning in and taking interest though strangely showing no fear.

'Here we go,' commented Tempest as he stepped over the shards of mirror to inspect the passageway beyond.

Dr Parrish straightened to his full height, ignoring Tempest as he answered the question. 'It is an ancient Incan tool for capturing the souls of their enemies. Back then, they would use still water to trap the soul, destroying it by throwing dirt into the puddle. Later, people learned to use mirrors. How would this beast know to set such a trap?'

The dwarf spoke up. 'Lord Hale, have your family ever had any dealings with Columbia or the Incas specifically?'

Lord Hale looked perplexed as he scoured his memory. 'I don't… maybe. It would have been generations ago. Do you think there might be a connection?'

While the men by the door discussed the Incan empire, the five women I hadn't yet met were beginning to chant in the far corner. I turned my attention their way and was about to move when Patience put out an arm to stop me. 'Don't disturb them, girl. What's wrong with you? Don't you recognise witches when you see them?' Five sets of piercing blue eyes all snapped up to look in our direction. 'Oh, my gosh!' squeaked Patience. 'I think I pissed them off.'

'Witches?' sneered Tempest's mum, Mary. 'Godless heathens.'

The chanting stopped and a bony finger pointed at her as the eldest of the five raised her right arm. 'Not godless. Different gods. Will your god grant you protection this night?'

'There is only one God,' Mary spat back at them. 'You ought to think about taking Jesus Christ as your saviour and stop worshipping horse gods with big whatnots or whatever weird nonsense it is you want to follow.'

Another of the women surged forward, only to be caught and held back by her companions. 'She insults us!' she raged.

Calmly, the elder witch, a slim woman in her late forties said, 'The uneducated always fear that which they cannot comprehend.'

'Let it be, Mary,' warned Tempest's dad.

I could see she had no intention of doing so but as she wound up to return a fresh verbal volley, I realised I was shivering again. 'Has anyone else noticed the temperature is dropping?' I asked. My breath was coming out in clouds suddenly.

Tempest stuck his head back through the door, huffed out a breath and looked down to the floor. I tracked his eyes so saw it too: a thick mist was rising from the floor. 'What's beneath this room?' he asked Lord Hale.

On the spot, Lord Hale didn't have an answer, 'Oh, I don't know. Actually, I'm not sure I have ever been in this part of the house before.'

'So, you cannot tell me what is on the other side of this wall, then?' Tempest pointed to his left and hefted a sledgehammer.

'Where the devil did you get that?' asked Dr Parrish in surprise.

'It was just lying around,' Tempest replied without bothering to look at him. 'Lord Hale?' he prompted.

'I'm not sure,' said Lord Hale, his brow wrinkling. 'What is it you are proposing?'

Tempest grasped the hammer with both hands as he stepped between Dr Parrish and Frank. 'To me, it feels like we are being led through this house. Every room we find ourselves in only has one way out. I think I would like to create a new way out.'

'Goodness me, no!' blurted Lord Hale, finally understanding what Tempest planned to do.

'Yeah, let's remodel!' cackled Big Ben, following Tempest as he lined himself up to a wall.

'No!' insisted Lord Hale. 'This is my ancestral home! No damaging it, please.'

Tempest turned around and put the hammer down, accosting Lord Hale with a frown. 'I thought you were about to be dead and desperate to have us save you? If you are to die tonight, why care about a little bit of redecoration for the new owners?'

Lord Hale let his shoulders slump. 'I suppose you are right. I want to explore a little further though, see if we cannot find our way back to a point in the house that I know. There's no point knocking through a wall to find it goes nowhere.'

Tempest couldn't argue with his logic or his request to delay the smashing, so he put the hammer over his shoulder and started back toward the door and the passageway beyond. 'Let's see where those stairs go shall we?'

He wasn't in the lead though. The elegant woman I saw in the bar earlier was, the one who had been drinking the Bloody Mary and watching everyone. I hadn't heard her speak yet, but she did now. 'I think we have wasted enough time talking. You say your name is Tempest?'

'It is,' Tempest replied.

'Good. Strong name for a strong man. Stick close to me please, I shall feel safer with you by my side.' I rolled my eyes. In all this craziness, the middle-aged socialite had time to flirt with my boyfriend, and he was trailing along beside her like an obedient dog.

Dr Parrish followed, with the dwarf, Lord Hale and Frank on his heels, then the five witches, Big Ben, Patience, Tempest's parents and me. I wondered how far Tempest would get before he thought to check I was still following.

The passageway went about thirty yards and then became a set of rickety, creaking, wooden stairs. Ahead of me, the group descended them using torchlight to see by. My phone was back in my clutch bag, but I could see enough and had no idea how long we would be creeping about in the dark. If other people's phone batteries started to die, I wanted mine to have juice left in it.

The stairs took us down and down. I didn't start to count until I realised we had gone down more than a floor's worth. We had been on the ground floor so were now somewhere beneath the house in the basement levels I saw labelled in the elevator. It finally levelled off, but we had to be two floors down, so did that mean we were now at the bottom?

The voices I could hear below me as I came down the last few steps were exclaiming about the mist following us. I turned around to see what they were talking about, but sure enough, the thick mist rising up from the floorboards in the creepy toy room was coming down the stairs toward me. It was impenetrable, light from torches below bouncing off it as it crept over another step to obscure it.

Tempest was pushing his way back through the crowd in the passageway below. 'Amanda, can you smell it?'

'Smell what?'

'No. I mean, can you take a whiff of the mist and tell if it is dry ice?' he clarified.

I had to question if I would know dry ice if I smelled it, but I suspected I would, so I went back up a few steps to scoop some of the thick mist. An itchy voice at the back of my head told me a hand was going to reach out of the mist any second now and grab me. If it did, I would honestly wet myself, but nothing happened as I sniffed at the mist cupped in my right hand. It was almost thick enough to bite but it wasn't dry ice. Or, at least, I didn't think it was.

'We should move on,' insisted Dr Parrish, his face appearing at the bottom of the stairs as he once again tried to lead the group.

I ignored him. 'I'm not sure what it is, but I don't think it's dry ice.' Tempest nodded and held out his hand for me to take as I descended the last few stairs. 'So what is it?' I asked. 'Any ideas?'

'None yet,' he admitted.

Then we heard his mother's voice. 'Tempest?' she called from the passageway the group were now congregated in. She sounded worried. 'Tempest?' she called much louder this time.

'Yes, Mother,' he answered, people trying to get to the side so he could pass. It was a log jam and his mother had moved to the front of the line, probably to put some distance between herself and the witches, but now she was staring at the elegant socialite and gripping her husband's arm for all it was worth. Pushing by Frank, there were still half a dozen people in the way. 'What is it, Mother?' he asked, a trace of impatience in his voice.

His mother held a trembling finger up and pointed to the wall opposite. Following her hand, I saw the wall was mostly a mirror. In the dark I hadn't noticed, but the length of the wall on that side was one giant mirror from about four feet up to about six feet. Looking at my reflection, I saw my hair was mussed up and I had cobwebs in it. That wasn't the most immediate problem though; the elegant socialite was. 'She's got no reflection,' Mary stammered, her finger wobbling as she stared.

Tempest saw it too. Right where his mother stood, her reflection and that of her husband as they looked at the mirror were clear, but the woman, whose back was to it, simply didn't appear in the mirror.

The woman smiled, then opened her mouth to reveal dangerous looking canine teeth as she hissed.

Tempest's mother screamed in surprise and the woman

lunged for her. His dad stepped in to deflect her, but she just swatted him away with a stiff arm. We were through the crowd now with just the dwarf and his axe in the way.

He raised it to block Tempest. 'She's a vampire!' he yelled. 'There's nothing you can do!'

Tempest said nothing and paid the dwarf no attention as he leapt into the air to sail right over his head. The sledgehammer, I realised, wasn't in his hands, so he must have put it down at some point, but he didn't need a weapon like that to deal with a crazy woman attacking his mum.

She already had hold of Mary but seeing Tempest coming, she hissed at him, pushed Mary away and ran, her elegant gown flapping behind her as she vanished into the dark.

Torches were all pointed down the passageway, but I was casting a big shadow as I ran after them with Tempest's dad at my side. The passageway came out into a large, empty room but now I couldn't see anything. Surely Tempest couldn't either, but rather than stumble blindly into something, I fished my phone out and got it working – just in time to see that Tempest was hurt.

Caught in the beam of light my phone cast, Tempest had blood coming from a wound on his head. He was hurt but before I could do anything, the vampire grabbed his arm and pulled him through a gap in the wall which then instantly closed and sealed.

Running footsteps behind me heralded the arrival of everyone else, including the elderly Lord Hale who was out of breath and clutching his heart. 'What happened?' asked Big Ben, looking around for Tempest as I clawed at the wall where he vanished.

'Give me a hand here!' I shouted, sparking him into

motion. He arrived at the wall a second later, Dr Parrish, Frank and others with him. 'He was hurt, I saw him bleeding, but Lady Emily pulled him through here and then it closed on them.'

'Where?' asked Dr Parrish, taking my claim seriously, but unable to see where the solid stone wall might have moved.

Nothing but a faint crack showed where the gap had been. 'It moved like a door,' I explained. 'As if hinged from the left edge. So, where I am pushing is the piece that will swing open.'

Big Ben didn't waste any time, grunting with effort as he heaved against the door, Tempest's dad joining in along with Frank but there was no more room to get anyone else in and their combined effort was doing exactly nothing.

'This thing's not going to move,' Big Ben concluded, adding a few extra words to emphasise his annoyance. 'We need a crowbar or something.'

'What about that sledgehammer?' suggested Tempest's dad. 'I'll get it.' He ducked back down the passageway to look for it while I did my best to resist kicking the wall in frustration.

Patience grabbed my arm, using it for support as she reached down. 'Girl, I have got to get these shoes off. They are not made for running around in.' I was wearing heels too. They went with the ballgown, and without them, the bottom three inches would drag along the floor and ruin. Cursing myself for caring when our situation was so dire, I looked down, using my phone to see, and expecting to find my dress already ruined from running about in a basement passageway. It wasn't though. The hem, which ended just an inch or so from the floor had no more than one or two small marks on it. Checking my dress, I noticed the floor itself. It was clean. Not just swept to remove the dust but actually clean as if someone had mopped it today. I wrinkled my forehead in wonder but looked up just as Tempest's father reappeared.

'It's not there,' he puffed, a little winded from running.

'He left it near the bottom of the stairs,' Mary provided helpfully.

Michael shook his head. 'That's what I'm telling you. It isn't there anymore. He put it down and someone took it.'

Angry, I swung my torch around, looking for whoever was holding onto it when we so clearly needed it. All I found was a sea of innocent faces though. No one had it. So where had it gone? I rounded on Lord Hale, wanting to grab him by his collar but holding back in deference to his age. 'Who was Lady Emily. What special set of skills warranted her invite?'

'Yeah,' echoed Big Ben.

Lord Hale gave me a look that suggested he thought I was being a bit thick. 'She's a vampire, my dear. She used to date my great, great grandfather back in their day and took his death at the hands of the monster quite personally. She has been waiting for her chance to even the score ever since.'

'Say what?' Patience wasn't buying it any more than I was.

Frank tutted in response though. 'I did tell you she was a vampire, Amanda.'

Ignoring him, I got in Lord Hale's face. 'Where is Tempest? Where does that door go?' Dr Parrish tried to take my arm, wanting to pull me away from our elderly host. I ripped it from his grip, snatching it away without breaking my focus on Lord Hale's face.

Dr Parrish cleared his throat. 'Perhaps we should move on.'

Now I turned my attention to him. 'Perhaps I should kick you in the nuts. Tempest just got dragged through that door and I, for one, intend to find him.' Michael echoed his support for finding Tempest, as did Big Ben and Frank.

Annoyingly, he used logic and reason against us. 'But there appears to be no way to follow. The wall is solid, so if your boyfriend did go through it…'

'I saw it close,' I growled through gritted teeth.

'Yes, yes. But no one else did.' He saw my murderous expression and tried again. 'Look, all I am saying is; if we cannot go that way, we waste time to continuing to stare at the wall. We should move on and find a way around.'

I was seething. However, there was no argument I could present at this time. Screwy things were happening; things I couldn't explain. The tension in the room became palpable though with Dr Parrish and I staring at each other and everyone else watching.

Big Ben whispered, 'He's pretty good at taking care of himself. He'll be fine. Of course, had it been me she grabbed, she and I would be getting down to it by now.'

In the dark, I heard Patience whack him on his head with her purse. 'Didn't you get enough earlier?'

'That was more than an hour ago, Patience,' he replied as if his comment explained everything.

Dismissing them as Patience took to idly threatening Big Ben, I glared at Dr Parrish and Lord Hale. 'Alright, we move on. I think you two are hiding something though. I think you know more than you are telling us and if I find out that is the case, there's going to be trouble.' I delivered my threat without the slightest hint of irony or humour. I wanted them to know I meant it.

Lord Hale's voice echoed in the dark as I pushed by him toward the dark hole in the corner that was our only way out. 'I can assure you, my dear, there is no…'

'Save it,' I snapped. The black hole was another dark passageway. This one though had a wooden door at the end of it.

Just as I set off, Big Ben stepped in front of me. 'I think I would like to lead now. Maybe whatever intends to leap out on us next would like a face full of me. That might change things up a bit.'

The whole group followed me into the passageway, Dr Parrish on my shoulder and Tempest's parents right behind him, Michael doing his best to give reassurance to Mary in the dark.

At the door, Big Ben paused, glanced back and then grabbed the door handle. 'Here goes nothing.'

The Body in the Library

I was watching Dr Parrish so when he tensed just before Big Ben opened the door, I saw it. Nothing happened for a second, the door swinging open to reveal a black void beyond, but then a chittering sound started within.

'What is that?' asked Patience, her voice trembling with obvious fear.

Whatever it was, I didn't like it and even Big Ben chose to hesitate at the door rather than go inside. Peering into the dark, the fluttering, chittering noise grew in volume and suddenly I knew what we were hearing.

Screaming, 'Get down!' I turned and threw myself against Patience, Mary and Michael, pushing them to the edge of the passageway as thousands of bats burst from the doorway. All around us, the dinner guests were screaming their surprise and horror, ducking to the floor to avoid being hit or entangled in the flying menace. The flock continued to swoop over us for five or six seconds before it began to trail off. I risked a glance just as the last few flew past and gingerly stood up again, offering Patience my hand to get her back on her feet.

She wasn't happy. 'I hate bats. Horrible little flappy mice that turn into vampires.'

'That's the spirit,' said Frank looking pleased. 'Although, in actuality, recorded instances of vampires turning into bats are a myth, something dreamed up by the…'

I held up a finger of warning. 'Stop talking, Frank.' Over my shoulder I called, 'Ben, what's in there?'

He had his phone out to shine around. 'It's a library. Doesn't look like anyone has been in here for decades, but there are books and scrolls and things everywhere.'

'Scrolls?' Gina piped up.

'Old books?' asked Professor Larkin. I looked back to find Frank rubbing his hands together and the academics peering around me to see what Big Ben had found.

Big Ben's voice echoed from the dark room, 'I lost my lighter somewhere, anyone got a match? I think I found some old lamps we can use.'

People started pushing around me, even Patience wanted to be out of the passageway and into somewhere a little roomier. Or maybe she just wanted to be near Big Ben. Soon I was the last one in the corridor, standing outside and looking in as I watched the group dynamics at play. There was something amiss, that was for sure and there had been since we arrived.

For starters, a house this size could not be maintained with four staff, especially given that the butler was so ancient and decrepit. Then the caterers had provided dinner but none of us had seen them at any point. Also, this place had a high-tech elevator, but it didn't have a router to provide basic internet and phone services? That wasn't right. Three of the group had gone missing now: the paranormal detective, Crouch, the wizard and now Tempest. Plus, Lady Emily the vampire if you could believe that. The monster had shown itself before we even got started with dinner and since then, Dr Parrish or the wizard had been trying to control where the dinner guests were going and how we should get there. Now we find ourselves in a library and I was willing to bet someone would find a clue to the Incan connection his family had.

Inside the library, a lamp sparked into life to illuminate the interior, then another, both of them held at head height to cast eerie shadows against the walls.

I kept my mouth shut as I continued to watch.

'I think we should be careful about what we touch and where we stand,' warned Dr Parrish. 'I am probably being overcautious but I, for one, will not be surprised to discover a booby trap of some kind down here.'

'Why?' I demanded, finally crossing the threshold to enter the room.

'Hmm?'

'Why would you think this place might be booby trapped, Dr Parrish? We haven't encountered any booby traps yet.'

Big Ben sniggered. When I shot him a look, he did it again. 'You said booby.'

I rolled my eyes and went back to staring at Dr Parrish. The dwarf stepped in between us, still carrying his big axe. 'I don't see what's so farfetched about that. Given all the events so far tonight, it seems like a logical precaution.' Before I could argue, there was an audible clicking sound and the door we came in through slammed shut behind us with a deafening boom that caused dust to sift down from the ceiling above.

'Oops!' We all turned to find Patience with her hand on

a book. It was halfway off a shelf but was stuck. 'I think this is connected to something.'

'Let me see,' said Dr Parrish, rushing to examine what she had found.

'It's a book about vampires and the author is Lady Emily Pinkerton,' Patience explained. 'When I saw it, I couldn't help but wonder if it had something to do with that crazy chick that grabbed Tempest.'

Lord Hale looked impressed, 'Quite so, quite so. Well done, that woman. You're the police officer, wot?'

'Patience Woods, M'Lord,' I thought for a moment she was going to curtsy, but if she was, I got in her way as I stuck my face in to see the book.

Dr Parrish stepped to his side to give me room and pointed behind the book. 'It's connected to a lever, you see? Quite ingenious.'

'Is it?' I cut my eyes at him. My boyfriend had just gone missing with blood coming from a wound on his head and he was all excited to find the group trapped in a library.

'I should think so,' agreed the dwarf who I noticed had a habit of defending everything Dr Parrish said. I squinted at him now, unable still to shake the feeling that I knew him from somewhere.

'That's all very nice,' growled Tempest's mother impatiently. 'But how do we get out now? I don't see any other doors and where is my little boy, hmmm? Where did he get to?' She looked overwhelmed by the night's events and about ready to burst into tears when she turned into her husband's chest and buried her face.

On the other side of the room, part watching proceedings and part poking around, the four professors were inspecting the contents of the room. The library was a large octagon, fitted with shelves containing books and rolled parchments, ornaments and objects and all manner of odd items that looked to have been collected from around the world. It was all covered in a thick layer of dust in direct contrast to all the corridors we had travelled through to get here. The shelves reached up way beyond head height. How one got to them, I could not fathom but then I saw a rail in the floor. 'What's this for,' I asked, pointing to the brass circle running all the way around the room.

'One thing at a time, my dear,' chuckled Dr Parrish as if I were being an overexcited woman. Mentally, I squeezed my fist shut imagining I had a part of his body in it that I was slowly crushing. At the rate he was going, I wouldn't be picturing it mentally for much longer. 'I think your friend has something here.' He was on his knees and fiddling with the book by Lady Emily Pinkerton that Patience found.

'Can't we open the door by putting it back?' asked Tempest's dad.

Patience shook her head. 'I tried that already.'

'I think I can disconnect it from the lever,' Dr Parrish managed between noises of concentration as he fiddled with something using one hand. He had to contort his body around to get his hand behind the book since it was connected somehow but wasn't having any luck doing whatever it was he was doing. 'I suspect it takes a deft touch,' he claimed in an apologetic manner.

Big Ben loomed over him. 'Let me try,' he offered, waving his fingers about in the air as if doing something magical and fancy. 'You would not believe what these fingers are capable of.'

Dr Parrish gave him a single raised eyebrow of confused disbelief and in response Big Ben clicked the thumb and middle finger of his left hand and Patience's bra came undone.

'Damn you,' she swore. 'I still don't know how you do that.'

As Patience fiddled around inside her dress to get her hands on the loose bra straps, Big Ben blew on his fingers like a wild west gunslinger and said, 'It's magic.' Then he cocked an eye at me. 'Want me to do yours?' I rolled my eyes and slapped his arm with my clutch bag. I wasn't wearing a bra but if I told him that he would probably offer to make my knickers fall off by blowing in my ear or something.

He looked down at Dr Parrish again, and this time Dr Parrish accepted defeat and moved out of Big Ben's way. Tempest's dad came to see if he could help. 'What've we got?' he asked, taking his glasses off to squint into the gap behind the book. 'Some kind of wired connection, linked to the bottom edge of the book, by the look of it.' He pulled a multitool from his pocket. 'I should have something on here we can undo the wire with.'

'Sure,' said Big Ben. 'Or...' he grabbed the book with one giant hand and ripped it free, 'we can just do that.' He tossed the book to Dr Parrish and leaned against the book-case. 'My friend is missing, and we are wasting too much time.' He said it like it was a threat.

The dwarf stepped in again. 'I can assure you we are all just as...'

'Uh, uh, uh,' Big Ben waggled a finger at him. 'That's quite enough from you, Tinkerbell. Pixies get to have an opinion later.'

The dwarf's mouth flapped open and closed a few times before his words caught up with his lips. 'A pixie?'

Patience smirked. 'Don't be getting all fiery now, he's just teasing.'

'Yes,' said Big Ben before the dwarf could reply. 'Just

teasing. Wouldn't want to offend a chap with a double headed axe.' He slapped the dwarf on the arm, which shunted him a foot to the right, and began to walk away. As he went, he murmured loud enough for everyone to hear, 'Besides, everyone knows Tinkerbell is a fairy.' As the dwarf lunged after Big Ben, Dr Parrish caught his shoulder and held him in check.

Lord Hale made sure he was between the dwarf and Big Ben as he held out his hands to see the book. 'This must be my great grandfather's collection,' he claimed. 'I knew he had pieces from all over but thought it to be lost. I doubt anyone has been in this part of the house in more than half a century and I never knew it existed.'

'How can that be?' I asked. His eyes swung in my direction. 'How can it be that you didn't know this was here. When was the lift shaft put in? It looks new, but whenever it was, they had to look at the plans for the building.'

He stretched out his bottom lip, pulling an expression to show that he didn't know the answer, 'I'm sure they did look at the plans, my dear. They being the contractors. I played no part in that and could have stared at the plans for a month without deciphering them. No, I'm afraid, my grandfather was something of an eccentric. He most likely squirrelled all this stuff away down here and kept it a secret from everyone.'

One of the professors asked, 'Do you think there might be some clues in here as to why the family carries this curse?'

Dr Parrish jabbed a finger in the man's direction. 'Good thinking that man. Everyone, start looking for anything to do with the Incas.' I screwed my face up in disbelief; it was starting to feel like I was in an elaborate escape room.

People were doing it though; the witches, the professors,

Dr Parrish and the dwarf; all of them were rummaging along the lines of books and artefacts as they looked for a clue.

'Should we be helping?' Patience asked.

I wriggled my lips as I thought. 'No. Leave them to their foolish errand. I am going to find a way out.' I pointed to the door we came in through. 'That's the only door, right?'

Behind me, Lord Hale, still reading from the vampire book by Lady Emily found something of interest. I stopped talking so I could hear what he had to say. 'This book is basically a memoir of the period she spent with my ancestor.'

I couldn't help myself from interrupting. 'I thought it was a book about vampires.'

'It is, my dear, it is. But Lady Emily wrote it as a memoir. Largely I think it is about being in love with my great, great grandfather and having to suppress her carnal urge to bite him all the time. A tale of unrequited love, if you like. In the passage I am reading, she makes reference to my great great grandfather's obsession with Incan mythology. He was to be the third Hale to be slaughtered by the monster if he made it to his eightieth birthday and spent much of his later years trying to work out what reason there was for the curse. I'll read you an extract.' Lord Hale cleared his throat as if about to give a speech and started reading. 'Rupert remains convinced the key to breaking the curse lies in his great grandfather's visit to Peru. He hasn't slept in days, smitten with the need to solve this puzzle. He fears not for himself but for future generations of Hales, most specifically focussing on his grandson, Eric, who will be the next victim of the monster if Rupert cannot stop his own death.'

As he burbled on, I continued listening but whispered

to Big Ben and Patience and started poking about for myself. The door shut when Patience triggered a lever, so it stood to reason that there had to be another lever to open it. The voice of doubt was screaming at the back of my skull, and it was certain the door was never going to open no matter what we did. This evening had been about moving us from one point to the next. So when we left this room, we would do so using a new door to the one we came in through. That might sound ridiculous in a room with only one door, but I also thought it would be entirely in keeping for us to find a secret passage behind a bookcase.

'How can we help?' asked Tempest's dad, looking eager to be doing something. He held his wife's hand in his, the two inseparable it seemed. I explained my thoughts about how we would be able to escape the room and pointed out the rail in the floor. Then we all split up and started to examine the bookcases, the books and objects on them. Somewhere in here there had to be another trigger. We looked like we were doing the same thing as Dr Parrish and his academics; I even got a thumbs up from him when he caught my eye. His crew were looking for some clue about the ancient nonsense that caused the monster to manifest, and I was happy to let them do it. I still wasn't buying into the monster story; it was just too farfetched even after what I had seen.

I hadn't got far with my search for a secret door when I almost tripped over Frank. He was kneeling on the floor. 'Frank, what are you doing?' I asked, waving my arms to rebalance myself.

His face was almost level with the floor, and he didn't look up when he spoke. 'I think we might be in trouble.'

'What have you found?' I asked with a resigned sigh.

He called out, 'Lyndon.' Then sat back onto his haunches, blinking up at me through his thick glasses.

Dr Parrish came rushing over to see what Frank wanted, a large dusty book in his hands. 'What is it, Frank?'

He made a worried face but didn't get up. 'I thought this was a brass ring for a ladder to move around on so one could access the upper shelves.'

'Yes,' replied Dr Parrish, looking mystified about where Frank was going. I thought that was the purpose of the brass ring too.

'Well, bad news, I'm afraid. It's got an additional ring of silver running just inside it and there are tiny runes inscribed all over it.' I wasn't sure what that meant, but I was fairly certain it was something bad from the way the colour drained from Dr Parrish's face. He glanced about the room nervously, his eyes darting here and there.

Patience drifted over to see what we were doing. 'Let me guess,' she said with unforced resignation. 'There's something coming to get us.'

Frank sighed as he heaved himself off the floor. 'We're standing in a giant summoning circle.'

'Which means…' I prompted him.

'That someone built this room specifically to trap and hold something large.'

'Or,' cut in Dr Parrish, 'to create a protective circle to hide in so the something large couldn't get to them.'

The two men locked eyes, realisation clearly dawning on both their faces. 'This was supposed to keep the monster out!' they both cried jubilantly. Their shout got the attention of everyone in the room.

One of the witches said, 'Did I just hear you say protection circle?'

Excitedly, Frank pointed to the brass ring embedded in

the stone floor. 'Look. Just inside the brass is a silver circle and it is engraved with runes.'

'Is it complete?' asked another of the witches, the one with the utterly straight blonde hair. Her question caused a frantic scramble as half a dozen people, Frank and Dr Parrish included, all got on their hands and knees to inspect the circle.

Each of them was reporting back to the others and getting more and more excited until Dr Parrish swore and raised his hand. 'There's a break in it. Right here and its almost half an inch.'

'What does that mean, Dr Parrish?' asked Lord Hale, a hopeful look on his face.

Dr Parrish held out a hand so the dwarf could help him up. 'The circle cannot be closed unless it is complete. We need to find silver to fill the gap.' He wasn't defeated for long though. 'Quick everyone; look for an ornament or artefact made from silver. Look for ivory too, ivory trinkets were often mounted in silver.'

His request generated another scramble as the dinner guests began picking through the things on the shelves. 'Don't feel like helping?' the dwarf asked when he noticed I hadn't moved. Patience, Big Ben, and the Michaels were all next to me as we considered our next move. It had nothing to do with finding silver, but since he asked, I gave him my attention. 'Where's the bat droppings?' His eyes widened a little as if panicked by the question, but I saw Gina turn her head my way. I swung my head to take in all the faces looking my way. 'Is nobody else curious? There were ten thousand bats in this room but there's no poop. Were they magical bats?'

Gina put down the ornament she was holding. 'Yeah. Where did they come from even? If there's no way out of this room, then how were they alive? What do they feed on and where have they been perching?' She pointed to the ceiling. 'There's nothing for them to hang from.'

I got in on the action. 'The corridors outside are spotless. Barely any cobwebs and no dust or dirt on the floor. Does the monster have a cleaner?' That question got a snigger from a few of the dinner guests. 'What are you not telling us, Lord Hale?'

The elderly lord looked quite taken aback by my question. 'My dear, I cannot imagine what you mean.'

I didn't get to ask the next question because a loud thump hit the ceiling and shifted more dust. As it filtered down, I saw Lord Hale, Dr Parrish, and the dwarf all exchange a worried look. The thump sounded like something hitting the ceiling; something soft, rather than something hard. It landed near one edge of the octagon, over by the witches, who took a step back when they heard the object above their heads shift. It must have come to rest half on the ceiling, half hanging over the edge because we all heard it slide down behind the bookcase on that side and land at floor level.

I had a fresh stack of questions to ask. I didn't ask any of them though, I walked to the bookcase where the something had just landed behind, took the books off it and thumped the wood at the back. I got a hollow sound.

'What was that?' asked one of the witches. She and her colleagues were still staring in the direction the object had landed. Whatever it was, was behind the bookcase, or behind the wall assuming there was a wall there. It didn't sound like there was.

'Ben,' I called to get his attention. 'It's action time.'

'Yeah, baby. Now we're talking.' He rubbed his hands together gleefully, very much the man of action and never happier than when he was either hitting something or getting naked.

'What are you doing?' asked Dr Parrish, trying to get in our way as we crossed the room to where the object had fallen. Using his body as a barrier wasn't a tactic that would work for very long with Big Ben around.

I pointed an accusing finger at him. 'I don't know what game you are playing, Dr Parrish, but it is clear we are being duped somehow. I am going to leave now. I don't know what just hit the floor behind the bookcase, but it sounded like a body to me.' There were several gasps at my statement. 'So there is clearly a cavity behind that bookcase, and I am willing to bet that it will prove to be the passageway we are supposed to find to get out of this room and onto the next bit of this odd and clearly fake experience.'

'Dr Parrish, what is going on?' asked Lord Hale. 'They act as if they don't know.'

'Don't know what?' asked Big Ben, sounding dangerously close to thumping someone.

'What you are doing here,' replied Lord Hale looking utterly perplexed. 'It was all on the invitations.'

'Yes, that's right,' agreed Dr Parrish. 'We are trialling a new high-ticket murder mystery escape room experience and asked you all to test it out for us and provide feedback. So far, I cannot fathom what we paid for because you have all been bonkers and aggressive. Especially you,' he finished, jabbing a finger at Big Ben and only just managing to dart out of the way when Big Ben tried to snap it off.

I glanced at Gina. She was rummaging in her handbag 'That's not what the invite says at all,' she stated.

'Yeah,' agreed everyone single one of the witches. 'The invitation was to attend a birthday party dinner and help you live through the weekend because a monster is going to drag you to hell.'

'Here it is.' Gina held the invitation aloft triumphantly and brought it across for everyone to crowd around. I breathed a sigh of relief because I couldn't remember what it said. When Tempest and Jane had read it, I had glanced over his shoulder, but the detail hadn't been important at the time.

Dr Parrish stared at it, his lips moving as he read it and again the colour drained from his face. 'What is this?' he asked. 'This isn't what I wrote.' He was shaking his head and brought both hands up to cup his face. 'Someone switched the invitations.'

The dwarf finally put down his axe. 'Who would do that?'

'Oh no.' The latest comment came from Frank. He looked utterly crestfallen. 'You mean none of it was real?' His eyes were on his supposed partner for the night, Dr Lyndon Parrish. Dr Parrish had no answer though. Frank hung his head and shook it sorrowfully. 'Tempest is going to have a field day with this.'

The room was clearly divided into those who were in on the secret and those who were invited here. So far I had Lord Hale, Dr Parrish and the dwarf pegged and suspected Crouch, the paranormal detective grabbed first had to be in on the ruse, and likewise Lady Emily Pinkerton. So, now I really wanted to know what happened to Tempest.

'Hold on, hold on, hold, on.' Patience was getting upset. Her hands were balled on her hips, and she had a scowl that could melt an iceberg. 'You mean to tell me that I have been starving all evening, terrified half out of my wits and walking around with damp panties because the bats scared me so much a little bit of pee came out, all because you tricked us into going through an escape room we knew nothing about?'

'That's not exactly the case,' protested Dr Parrish.

Big Ben showed him a fist. 'What is the case? Start talking or I unleash Mr Left and Mr Right.' He brought his other fist up to join the first, convincing Dr Parrish to back away.

'I told you,' he continued to protest as he tried to hide behind the dwarf. 'You were supposed to know exactly what this weekend was. Lord Hale has spent a fortune developing the house to make it the ultimate escape room combined with a murder mystery.'

'We are aiming at the very top end of the market,' added Lord Hale. 'This will be where rock stars and footballers come for the weekend, enjoying a full immersion experience. It has been the work of many years to get the house ready. You were expected to tell us whether it was realistic or not. Too scary, not scary enough. We hired professional actors, spent a fortune on special effects, and are all set up to receive guests the week before Christmas, so this was a final run through to make sure everything worked as planned.'

I folded my arms to stop me waving them around angrily or succumbing to my base desire to thump someone. 'I think it's time we returned to the main house, don't you? Perhaps then, we can discuss how we came to know nothing about all this, and you can tell me where Tempest is.'

He took a step back to get to the bookcase where the object had fallen. 'Of course,' he replied. 'It's not far from here. I shall have the caterers provide drinks and food. Don't worry about Tempest though, I got a message from Anne,' he paused. 'Sorry, you know her as Lady Emily, but she's another actor hired to take on the role of the vampire among the dinner guests. She said he hit his head and she was taking him to the control room to get it looked at. He'll meet us upstairs most likely.'

'Hi, I'm Ronald,' said the dwarf. 'I'm an actor too.' He was smiling now, cheerful and excited about the role he was playing. 'Actually,' he went on, 'you might know me from a few television roles.'

'I knew I recognised you,' bragged Patience.

'He was R2D2?' asked Big Ben.

The dwarf scowled at him. 'I was in…'

'Happy Tunes Time,' provided Patience. 'I watched you all the time as a kid.'

While Ronald talked about what other shows he had done, Dr Parrish crossed the room, reached into the book-case and pulled a lever. With an audible click and a shifting of dust, it slid into the ceiling.

As it lifted, it revealed the object that hit the ceiling and fell down. Two of the witches screamed and jumped back, but everyone in the room got a shock as we saw the mangled body of Caratacus Soulful the wizard.

Big Problem

Lord Hale took a step forward, but I caught his arm. 'We have actual police with us and that's a dead body.'

'You think he's dead?' he gasped. I looked back down at the body and back up at Lord Hale's face. The wizard's head was on backwards, his neck rotated through one hundred and eighty degrees. I had no doubt at all that he was very dead indeed. Everyone else was peering at the body, but no one was going near it, the dinner guests forming a semi-circle around the entrance to the new passage. I crouched down to check his pulse, finding, as expected, that life had long since departed our fake wizard. 'What was his name?' I asked.

Dr Parrish answered, 'Kevin McHugh. He was a street magician we picked up in London a few months back. Since then he has been perfecting the role. His job was to lead us from the dining room and then give the suggestion of demonic powers at work when he was sucked into the mirror. The special effects work brilliantly in my opinion.'

'Well, they convinced me,' said Frank, still looking

despondent that we were not all going to meet our doom as the monster promised.

From his jacket pocket, Dr Parrish pulled a small two-way radio. He switched it on, checked the light on top and started talking into it. 'Dave? Dave are you there? This is Lyndon. We're in the library. There's been an accident. Can you turn all the power and lights on, please? Over.'

No answer came back. Beside me Patience was grumbling, 'They had light down here the whole time but didn't turn it on. This place is getting a one-star review, make no mistake.'

Dr Parrish tried again. 'Hello, Dave?' Nothing. 'Hello, anyone in the control room, this is the main party in the library we need assistance. Over.'

Finally, the radio crackled at the other end, and we heard a rasping breath. When the voice spoke, it was the same voice of the monster we heard in the dining room. 'You will all perish here this night.'

The person at the other end released the send switch and was gone. 'Hello?' called Dr Parrish. 'Hello?'

'Here, let me try,' insisted Lord Hale, taking the radio from Dr Parrish's hand and doing the exact same thing with the exact same results.

I was beginning to get a bad feeling in my stomach. There was nothing we could do for Kevin McHugh. We didn't even have a blanket or a sheet to cover him with, but we couldn't stay here, and we shouldn't move him.

I stepped over the body, straddling it with my legs and beckoning for the dinner guests to start down the passage-way. 'We have to move on.' My comment was aimed at Dr Parrish and Lord Hale who were now bickering about whether Dr Parrish was using the radio right or had put the right batteries in it.

'It must have the right batteries in,' protested Dr Parrish. 'Otherwise, it wouldn't work at all. Those idiots in the control room are just playing a trick on us. When I get hold of them...'

'It's not much of a trick,' Tempest's dad pointed out. 'Someone is already dead.' He paused in front of Lord Hale. 'Am I safe to assume you know the way out of here?'

'Of course...'

'And there'll be no more surprises?' Michael Michaels wasn't as imposing as his son, but he had been in the forces for many years, so despite his advancing years, he was quite able to stare a man down.

Lord Hale made sure there was no humour in his voice when he said, 'I shall take you directly back to the accommodation area of the house.'

'Jolly good,' replied Tempest's mother. 'You might want to call ahead and make sure the gin is chilled.'

A shout echoed back down the passage, drawing my attention as the last of the dinner guests filed out of the room. Ronald had elected to lead us, using one of the lamps from the library to light the way. 'It's Brian,' he announced, looking back toward Lord Hale and Dr Parrish. 'He came to find us.'

As he turned around again and held up the light, what emerged from the darkness of the passageway was the monster; all spindly arms and giant body. Its eyes glowed orange still and it was just as terrifying to look at now as it had been earlier.

'Brian,' Ronald started to say, 'any idea what's going on in the control room?' I think he had more to say, probably intending to tell Brian we had just found Kevin, but Brian jabbed out with one of his spindly arms and skewered Ronald where he stood.

Ronald said, 'Ack,' flailed his arms a bit and dropped the lamp. We all watched it in mute horror, too stunned to react until the lamp smashed and their end of the corridor was plunged into darkness again.

Big Ben was the first to react, yelling like an enraged bear as he charged forward, casting fresh light with his phone as he went. I was hot on his heels with Frank and Tempest's dad, but when we got to Ronald's body, the monster was already gone. Disappeared back down the corridor or through another hidden door. No sooner had I questioned where he might have gone, than the clang of a door echoed back along the dark corridor.

Yet again I shoved myself into Lord Hale's face, unable to keep the anger down any longer. 'What the hell is going on?' I demanded. 'That man is dead, and we just watched him get killed by your supposed monster. Who is inside the suit?'

'I… I… I don't know what's happening,' he stammered, completely caught off balance by the turn of events. 'I told them we were coming out now. You heard us call the control room.'

'Who is inside the suit?' I demanded again.

'Brian Carruthers. It should be Brian Carruthers. We hired him from…' I cut him off with an angry sneer and snatched the radio from his hand.

Jabbing the send switch with my thumb, I growled into the mouthpiece, 'Whoever is in this house that can hear me. You picked on the wrong group of people. I want my boyfriend back and as of right now, I don't care who you are. You have one chance to turn the power back on and run away.' I waited three seconds. 'Too late. Now I'm coming for you. You can hide in the dark, but I'm going to find you.'

75

I slapped the radio back into Lord Hale's hand.

Patience said, 'Damn, girl. That was scary. I'm gonna remember never to sleep with any of your boyfriends.'

'What's our move?' asked Big Ben. He had been kneeling over Ronald, but he was clearly dead which gave us two dead actors less than thirty yards apart.

I shone my phone's torch down the passageway. 'Can we get out that way?'

Dr Parrish and Lord Hale pushed around me in the narrow corridor. 'Yes, this is the way out. It leads to the elevator,' announced Dr Parrish, trying to be in charge again. I wasn't going to oppose him; I needed his knowledge to find the fastest way out. After that, I was going to track down whoever was behind the murders and find Tempest.

Big Ben went with them, leaving me to wait for the other guests to catch up. They were spread out along the corridor, many of them, Tempest's mum especially, not wanting to step over, or even get near to, the bodies. There was little choice if we wanted to get out.

However, no sooner had I helped Mary to step over the fallen dwarf, Ronald, and his growing pool of blood, than the sound of expletives echoed back along the passageway: Big Ben was upset about something. An angry rattling noise reached our ears followed by more interesting expletives and then the sound of footsteps coming back in our direction. Big Ben emerged from the gloom, deliberately not using his torch because it would blind us as he approached.

'The door is locked and probably barred from the other side,' he announced in a grumbling, angry voice before any of us could ask. 'We are not getting out that way.'

'But,' stammered Patience, 'but, I thought that was the only way out? That's what the old man said.'

'That's right,' Dr Parrish nodded. 'We designed it as a

route with very few extra ways out. The secret doors and escape passages, like the one Anne led Tempest into, are all operated by the people in the control room but have switches in the passageway as well. Anne did her bit on cue and was supposed to escape through the hidden door to reappear later. When Tempest hit his head, she took him to get some first aid assistance. In hindsight, we could all have got out through that door, but now we are cut off from it.'

'So we're trapped here?' asked a witch, clearly disturbed by the idea and fighting her rising terror. 'How far underground are we?'

It was a good question, but I had a better one. 'What's above the library?'

Escape

I pushed those behind me back into the library. We had all stopped in the tight passageway between the two bodies but with no hope of escape that way, there was no point in staying there any longer.

There were more lamps in the octagonal room, so we lit those, matches from one of the witches coming in handy. 'Kevin's body fell from somewhere. We all heard it, right? So, what's above the ceiling?' I pointed up as I asked the question. Lord Hale wasn't much help in providing an answer, but I think he genuinely didn't know. He was fiddling with his phone and looked agitated that no answer was coming back. The same thing with the radio as he continually attempted to raise the control room or anyone else and got no response.

Big Ben looked up at the ceiling, glanced around the room and shucked his dinner jacket. 'I'll get on it. I need something to climb on.'

'How about this?' asked Professor Pope, tapping a huge wooden chest with his foot.

I hadn't noticed it before. 'What's in it?'

He lifted the lid. 'Nothing. It's just a big chest.'

Big Ben sniggered. 'I think the table is a better bet. That ceiling is pretty high.' As he started dragging the table across the room with Tempest's dad, Frank and others helping, I started to mentally note what I knew. It got confusing though, so I grabbed a book. 'Anyone got a pen?'

'Um, here, love,' said Mary, rummaging around in her handbag. She couldn't find it so started taking things out and dumping them on the table Big Ben had climbed onto. Out came a crumpled pack of indigestion tablets, a ball of wool with two knitting needles through it and a half-finished baby jumper.

'Who's that for?' asked Patience, grinning at me in the lamp light. I cut my eyes at her.

In response Mary continued rummaging but said, 'I'm not getting any younger.' She left it at that thankfully; now was not the time for a conversation about babies with my boyfriend's mother. I already knew her stance on the subject and wondered how many pairs of knitted booties she had already made in the few weeks Tempest and I had been dating. 'Here it is,' she announced, pulling an old Bic biro from the bottom of the bag. 'Michael likes to do sudoku but is always losing his pens.'

With the pen in hand and Patience holding a phone for me to see, I started jotting bullet points:

- Someone doctored the invitations so we wouldn't know this was a trial run of an escape room.
- Tempest is missing and would have returned by now if he were able. The moment he found out it was fake he would have gone nuts.

- There's no answer in the control room, so either all or some of the staff are up to something.
  - What happened to the staff that are not involved if there are any?
- Two people are dead. There may be more so there is a killer loose. Is that all this is, and if so, what is motivating it?
- What likely motivations are there?

'Lord Hale,' I called. He was helping Big Ben and most of the others to stack books under the table's feet to make it higher.

'Yes, my dear?'

'How many staff are working here? It is obviously not the four that Travis claimed.'

'Goodness no. I, ah, I'm not sure actually. Dr Parrish?'

'Yes?' Dr Parrish was also chipping in, helping to carry more books to the table.

'Dr Parrish, how many staff are working here?'

'That depends,' he replied, cryptic as usual and not very helpful.

'What does it depend on?' I asked sweetly, hoping he would understand I might stab him with the biro if I didn't get a straight answer.

'Time of day and why you want the information.' Before I could rise from my chair to shout in his face, he kept talking. 'There are forty-three in total if you include everyone on payroll. The caterers will have gone home by now though, less the house cook who lives on site. Brian, Kevin, Ronald, and Anne plus myself and of course Derek.'

'Who is Derek?' I asked.

'That's the chap who played Mortimer Crouch. He's not

really an actor. He runs the control room with Dave, but we needed someone who would be grabbed by the monster right at the start before we got on with all the real special effects. He then runs back to the control room. It was cheaper than hiring another actor just for that quick stint.'

'Please continue,' I prompted, trying to steer him back onto the topic at hand.

'Yes. Yes, sorry. Where was I? Oh, yes; six of us make up the in-role team as dinner guests plus Dave in the control room. So, in the house right now should be,' he had to use his hands to count. 'So, that's ten?' he asked Lord Hale for confirmation.

'Plus Travis,' Lord Hale added.

'Eleven then,' I concluded. 'Of those people, two are already dead. We need to ask ourselves why?'

Lord Hale bore a confused face. 'Isn't that a job for the police?' he asked.

Patience leaned in. 'Sweetie, I am the police. I left my cuffs in the room, which is a good thing for you two because I feel like arresting someone for killing my feet.' She stared at them. 'You hear me. My feet are killing me! You two killed my feet. That's foot murder right there. Not to mention the state of my dress now.'

Ignoring her ramblings, I closed the book. Writing my thoughts down helped to get it clear in my head. 'Someone wanted us trapped down here. That much should be clear to all of us, so the question is, who and why. Why are two men dead? Did Kevin stumble onto something after he left us? If so, did the same thing happen to Derek and that's why there is no answer from the control room? We are trying to escape this trap they have us in, but I want to know what awaits us when we do.'

'That ought to do it,' Tempest's dad said as he lined the table up again. Each foot was balanced on a pile of books almost three feet tall. It looked precarious, Big Ben clearly sharing my opinion as he climbed carefully on top of it. Everyone with a torch lit shone it toward the ceiling high above.

Big Ben stands six feet seven inches tall in his socks so on top of a table boosted up by three feet of books he was able, with his stupidly long arms, to reach about sixteen feet into the air. This was a good thing because the ceiling was still more than two feet above his outstretched fingers.

'Now for the fun bit,' he murmured grimly. I wondered what he meant until he bent his knees and threw himself upward. As he reached the apex of his leap, he punched upward to strike the ceiling, smashing a hole through it with his meaty right first. He landed again, the table wobbling even with ten people holding it firm.

Bits of plaster fell to coat his hair and clothes and face. Ignoring it, he dipped his knees and thrust upwards again. With a few more attempts, there was a sizeable hole, and he had found a truss running along on the other side of the plaster board.

With his next leap, he grabbed it with both hands, performed a muscle up and disappeared through the hole.

Every face in the room was turned to look upwards. His phone torch came on, piercing the darkness in the ceiling void as he shone it around and his voice echoed as he called back down to us. 'The void goes straight up. My torch isn't powerful enough to see all the way to wherever the top is, but if that Kevin fella fell from the top, it's no wonder he didn't survive. I think there's a crawl space ahead of me so I'm going to explore that.' Several of the witches wished him good luck, Patience narrowing her eyes at them though they didn't see it.

We all waited in silence for his return, able to track his progress from the sound of his shoes on the roof trusses. When his head finally reappeared, he was filthy, covered in cobwebs and dirty from the dust mixing in his sweat. 'There is a crawl space. It heads in the direction of the passageway with the barred door, but I'm too big to fit in it. Same problem I have with petite girls,' he added quite unnecessarily. 'I need someone small.'

'I'll go,' said the blonde witch with the straight hair.

'Pick me,' insisted another. 'I've got tiny hips.'

Patience grabbed Frank by his jacket collar. 'Here you go, Benjamin. One volunteer.' I knew why she did it, I would have done the same, but Frank was arguably the smallest in the room anyway.

It took a bit of juggling and balancing. Frank was never going to be able to reach the hole, and they dare not stack any more books under the legs. So three men climbed onto the table: Tempest's dad and Dr Parrish both giving Frank a boost to get him high enough to reach Big Ben's outstretched arm.

Big Ben was lying down over the roof trusses and now had Frank dangling in mid-air from one hand. 'Ready?' he asked, but he didn't wait for an answer, he just yanked Frank up through the hole in one fluid motion, Frank giving a little wail of concern as he vanished through the dark hole. Safely up, Big Ben poked his head back through. Looking at the witches, he said, 'I think it would be better to send two, just in…'

'No. One will do just fine,' insisted Patience, glaring at the eager witches until they saw her and averted their eyes.

Big Ben's chuckle echoed back through from the void as

he disappeared. Then we could hear his voice and Frank's voice but couldn't make out what either was saying.

By my ear, Tempest's dad said in a hushed voice, 'Do you remember the scene in *Alien* when the captain goes into the tunnel to flush out the creature?'

A lump formed in the pit of my stomach.

Frank

There was nothing to do but fret while we waited for Frank to reappear, no way of knowing if the crawl space he went into would lead him anywhere helpful or how long it might take to get there. With all that in mind, I gave in and sat myself down on the floor.

Patience saw me and flopped down next to me, her arm touching mine. 'All things considered, Amanda, I wish I had stayed at home.' I couldn't offer much in the way of argument – I felt the same. Mostly I was trying to keep a lid on my worry over Tempest. His father was staying strong, trusting his son to find a way to be okay. Tempest's mother, however, was not doing very well so any sign of doubt on my part might tip her over the edge.

We were all in the octagonal library, waiting for Frank to find his way safely to the other side of the door and then hopefully find a way to open it. The monster had to have ducked back out of it before barring it, or locking it, or whatever trick the person inside the suit had used to prevent our escape, so another concern was that the killer might still

85

be hanging around. Tempest talked about Frank as if the small man were a warrior or something; he said he had the heart of a lion. Nevertheless, he wasn't armed and there was no doubt the person he might face was capable of killing.

Most of the dinner guests were milling about, doing very little and chatting among themselves, thankful we had light still.

'How much juice is in your phone?' I asked Patience, leaning my head her way to see.

She popped her clutch open to take it out. 'Twenty three percent battery. It was fully charged not long ago.'

'Using the torch always kills the battery,' I commented. I didn't check mine, but I doubted it was much better. The lamps were all in use, which might prove to be a mistake; we had no more paraffin, or whatever they worked on, to refill them and ought to be conserving what we had by only using one at a time, not the four we had currently illuminating the room.

Across the room, Gina and her fellow professors were still poring through books and manuscripts. I couldn't understand why since we had already proven the whole monster story to be a ruse, but they were distracting themselves and doing no one any harm so there was no reason to disturb them.

Gina chose to disturb us though, the volume of their conversation creeping up as they became more animated. It didn't take long for others to become interested, Dr Parrish taking it upon himself to get involved again. 'Is something the matter?' he asked.

Professor Wiseman stopped mid-sentence, glanced down at the large book Gina held and poked a finger at a page.

'How much of the assembled garbage in this room is props and how much is genuine?'

The question caught Dr Parrish by surprise, stuttering as he looked about at the shelves, he said, 'I, ah, I think it is all props.'

'There,' concluded Professor Wiseman to his colleagues, 'I told you so.'

Gina wasn't convinced though. She turned the book around so she could show it to Dr Parrish, balancing it against a shelf because it was heavy. 'This book was published in 1834 and it's not a case of faking it by making it now and putting an old first-published date in it; the paper in the book is Chaucer's old fine made by Eton Bond. Look – you can see the water mark.' Gina held it up for all to see and a few politely curious faces peered where she was pointing, though I was sure what they saw meant nothing to them.

Professor Pope got it though. 'It really is that old.' When he saw that no one else followed, he explained. 'Chaucer's old fine was really high-end stuff, too expensive by far for today's market. The last mill able to produce it went out of business in the last century.'

They thought they were on to something, and I was starting to find myself interested. Patience not so much which she confirmed by quietly grumbling, 'Those guys need to get laid. They have way too much free time for studying.'

Dr Parrish had screwed up his face in confusion. 'So, it's old paper. Why is that interesting?'

Gina gave him a patient smile but flicked her eyes to Lord Hale. 'Because our host recently claimed the monster and the entire tale was fabricated.'

'Yes. It was,' Dr Parrish defended.

Gina pointed to the text again. 'Not according to this it wasn't. The whole story, almost to the word is recorded here.'

Lord Hale looked very guilty when every pair of eyes in the room swung in his direction. He had been fiddling with his phone and getting more frustrated that it wouldn't do whatever it was he wanted it to do, now he was aware that we were all staring at him. Struggling to find a lie, he said, 'I had to base the story on something, so I used old family legends. It's all utter tosh of course.'

Gina shook her head. 'I'm not so sure it is.' Now that she had the attention of the crowd, she started to explain. 'This book was written by Lord Hale and published in 1834. That would make him… what? Your great, great, great grandfather? He would have been one of the genera- tions the curse skipped. He gathered evidence of the monster's visitation. Eyewitness records from staff. Did you know that it wasn't only the Lord Hales who were killed by the monster? Every person that attempted to intervene was killed too. I'll read you a passage.'

Gina cleared her throat. 'The great house is sombre this morning. Lord Hale, my father, was killed last night by the very thing he did all he could to prevent. His butler, Swale, and three footmen defended him with rifles but to no avail as the monster claimed them all. Alas, he considered me too vital to risk and ensured my commanding officer assigned me to duty at Horse Guards in London. I return home today to find my ancestral home in mourning. I make it my vow to investigate this curse so that it will not befall my eldest son, Gideon.' She looked back up to meet our faces. 'This is real. Whether you want to believe it or not, there really is a monster plaguing this house.'

No sooner did she make that announcement, than a low

moaning noise just like the one we heard in the dining room began. At first, I couldn't pinpoint where it was coming from, but air coming through the hole in the ceiling drew my eyes upward. A rush of wind flapped the tattered edges of the ceiling tiles and rattled the books and manuscripts on the shelves. Tempest's mum crossed herself again, an action that seemed to be having little positive effect, and the witches began chanting once more.

'Is this another one of your tricks?' I shouted at Lord Hale, making no effort to conceal the warning my words contained.

He held up his phone with an exasperated gesture. Then took the little radio from his pocket and held that up too. 'I am cut off from everyone. They're supposed to let us out when I call them.'

The moan grew louder, the wind too as it buffeted my hair and made me cold. I jumped when an enormous figure came hurtling through the hole in the ceiling to crash into the table. It was just Big Ben though, looking filthy and yet still dashing when he flashed the room a smile. 'Don't worry, ladies; I am here. Hoorah!' He took a second to flamboyantly pose atop the table with his hands on his hips like he was a superhero, then jumped down with a two-footed landing to accidentally bump into most of the witches.

Patience cracked her knuckles.

Big Ben's tomfoolery lightened the mood for a split second, but it dipped sharply when something heavy smashed into the ceiling and left a dent. I ducked automatically, an involuntary reaction to my brain telling me the roof was about to cave in. It held but then the heavy something started to walk across the roof, and it was heading toward the hole.

All any of us could do was watch the hole and wait.

However, when I realised that was what I was doing, I pulled my mouth into an angry sneer and moved toward the centre of the room.

'Girl, are you crazy?' yelled Patience.

The wind was gone and the moan, which built to a crescendo, stopped when the heavy thing hit the ceiling. It was quiet when the monster's voice called out. 'Lord Hale, it is time. Come forth so that no others need die in your stead.'

It was Tempest's father who spoke first. 'I thought we all just decided that we were in an escape room and the monster story was all made up.'

Gina shook her head sadly. 'Invented, yes, but taken from real family legends that appear to have a basis of truth.'

'Dr Parrish,' Lord Hale stuttered nervously. 'Dr Parrish, what do you have? I hired you because of your expertise in this field.'

Dr Parrish was fiddling with an inside pocket. 'Goodness, I could do with Frank right now.' He shot a look at the witches as he crouched down to unfold a handkerchief. 'Ladies can you be ready with a binding charm?'

'We are earth witches,' their leader replied. 'We can only enhance and guide that which mother earth grants the world. Binding belongs in the dark arts,' she chided as if talking to a beast.

'Perfect,' muttered Dr Parrish. 'I'll do it the hard way then.'

'Bored,' announced Big Ben, jumping back onto the table and standing so his head was directly underneath the hole. 'Hey, monster. Come down here and fight. I'll even let you have first hit.'

The voice from above chuckled, a deeply awful sound

which was followed by a disgusting, spindly limb shooting through the hole. Big Ben saw it coming but couldn't get out of the way fast enough to stop it snagging his left shoulder. A spray of blood hit the floor near my feet as Big Ben tumbled off the table.

'I shall return, Lord Hale,' rasped the voice through the hole. Silence reigned for several seconds, only to be replaced by the sound of Dr Parrish berating Big Ben for ruining his big moment. 'You utter fool. I could have wounded him and bound him to this house.' He jabbed a finger at the handkerchief in his right hand. 'Do you know what these are?'

Big Ben guessed, 'Yesterday's sneezes?'

The blonde witch rushed across the room to his aid. 'You're bleeding.'

'It's just a scratch,' he lied, blood now soaking the upper part of his shirt sleeve.

Unperturbed by Big Ben's injury, Dr Parrish sneered in his face. 'These are shards of a dawn's sunbeams. They cost more than you earn in a year, and they would have injured the beast if I could have got into position, you great oaf.'

Big Ben reached up to grab a handful of blood-soaked sleeve and ripped it off from the shoulder seam with yank. It exposed the wound for all to see. Then, just as Dr Parrish was carefully folding the handkerchief again, Big Ben grabbed it and used it to stem the flow of blood.

'Whaaa!' cried Dr Parrish but too late the precious cargo it supposedly contained was ruined forever.

Big Ben tipped him a wink. 'Thanks, pal.'

The blonde witch was making herself useful, trying to get a look at the wound and not lick her lips too much as she handled his muscular arm. In the very top of his deltoid was a stab wound as if the monster's paw ended with a knife. It was the same with poor Ronald who had run onto the monster's weapon. Big Ben would survive though, the wound bad enough to leave a scar but no danger to his life.

'We need more bandages,' said the witch as she shucked her jacket and pulled up her skirts to get to the material beneath. That it exposed her toned, shapely legs all the way up to her upper thigh was no accident. It caught Big Ben's attention, as she intended it to, but as she bent over to rip a piece of material from inside her skirt and in so doing made sure her breasts were hanging almost out of her top, Patience gave her a rough shove and knocked her over.

'Excuse me, sugar,' she said sweetly. 'Large, black woman coming through.'

I had to admit I was entertained but a thought shot through me suddenly as I remembered something I should never have been able to forget. 'Frank's out there!'

Where is Lord Hale?

SUNDAY, DECEMBER 11TH 0004HRS

My pulse spiked as I ran to the passageway, snatching a lamp as I went and jumping over Kevin's body in my haste. Dr Parrish came with me, both of us running, though Dr Parrish saw our separation from the group as a chance to air a grievance. 'I really don't like your big friend.'

Now wasn't the time and I was the wrong person to tell. What did he think I was going to do about it? Big Ben was a nightmare, but he was also great to have around if a problem presented itself that could be solved by beating everyone up, or by seducing a whole line of women. I didn't bother to answer though because a loud banging started ahead of us.

It sounded exactly like someone knocking urgently to be let in. Before we got there, my lamp held high to see what was ahead, Frank's voice started. 'Hey! Hey, inside, let me in.' His wail confused me as I thought it was locked on his side.

'We're coming, Frank!' I yelled back, quickening my pace to get there for him. He sounded terrified.

In response I heard a panicked, 'There's something coming.' Then I reached the door, a big wooden thing with a throw bolt in the middle. I threw the bolt and yanked the door open, Frank tumbling in and bumping into me, his face bounding off my left boob in the dark. Then he pushed off me and slammed the door shut again. 'It's coming!' he gibbered.

I had only seen the other side of the door for a split second, but I saw the large iron bolts fitted top and bottom. If we didn't open the door now, whoever was out there could just lock us in again and I doubted Frank wanted a second trip through the crawl space.

Gulping down my fear, I pushed myself in front of Frank and opened the door.

'What are you doing?' squeaked Frank.

'Close the door, woman,' demanded Dr Parrish, which got him a fast, raised eyebrow he probably couldn't see. If he called me woman again, we were going to have words.

I stood my ground, keeping my legs tensed in case I needed to move, but no monster appeared from the gloom on the other side.

'Can we get out of here now?' asked Tempest's mother. I turned to find everyone had followed us from the library and were looking eager to find a way out. 'I have had enough of the dark and there has to be some decent wine to drink in a house this size.'

Her husband said, 'I thought you wanted to go home?'

'And I'll be taking the wine with me,' she snapped.

I couldn't blame her for wanting to leave. As soon as I found Tempest, I would do the same. There were two murder victims here though, so someone had to stay and deal with the police, but regardless of any of that, we first had to actually find a way out. I held the lamp high and stepped through the door. Nothing skewered me, though my heart beat hard in my chest as I swung the lamp in each direction and half expected it to reveal a snarling row of giant teeth bearing down on my head.

I was moving slowly, which invited conversation. Dr Parrish asked Frank what he had seen. 'Seen?' he echoed. 'I didn't see it. I found my way through the conduit by luck more than anything, guessing which way to go. It was filled with electrical cable and ventilation pipes so I was lucky I could squeeze through at all.'

'I said I wouldn't fit,' Big Ben reminded us.

'So, what do you think it was?' asked the blonde witch. 'What did it sound like?'

Frank took a second, then blew out a hard breath before he spoke. 'I think it was the monster again. When I was most of the way through the crawl space, a terrible wind stared pushing dust and goodness knows what around and into my face. There was a terrible moaning sound.'

'We heard it too,' Dr Parrish assured him.

'Then I found a ventilation panel and could see a corridor on the other side. I had to knock the panel out with my head and then dive to the floor face first so I think it was talking but I really couldn't hear what it was saying.'

'It was threatening Lord Hale,' explained Dr Parrish. 'I was going to fight it...'

'With the captured dawn?' asked Frank, his excitement obvious. 'I have always wanted to see what it would do to a demon.'

'Well, I would have used it, but it met with a little accident and the monster escaped.'

'What happened to it?' Frank wanted to know.

'A great big…' Big Ben growled in the darkness. 'I'll tell you later,' Dr Parrish concluded.

Lord Hale's voice cut through the quiet. It was the first time he had spoken in ages. 'When we reach the junction ahead, the elevator is just along to the right. Make sure you turn right not left.'

I can admit I breathed a sigh of relief at that news. Getting out of the basement wasn't the same as escaping the house but it would feel like we were getting somewhere. At least we could access the rest of the house and maybe find out why the control room crew were not talking to us.

The moment I turned the corner, I knew my hopes were dashed again. The elevator, visible because I had the lamp in front of me and also because it looked like an elevator unlike the one on the ground floor, was dead. The call button, which I was sure should have a glowing light behind it, was just as dark as the rest of the basement. Even so, I paused in front of the door to futilely jab the button.

Tempest's dad asked, 'Problem?'

'No power to the elevator,' I called back, feeling despondent and trying to not sound it.

After a few seconds of silence, he said, 'I can fix that.' The dinner guests nearest me parted to let him through, Mary still on his shoulder as he fumbled in his pockets and produced a multi-tool. 'I never leave home without it,' he said brightly as he held it up to the light.

'He never does,' agreed Mary, though it was clear from her tone that she didn't consider it a good thing.

'Will he be able to fix it?' asked a witch.

I was getting fed up not knowing their names. They hadn't felt the need to introduce themselves at any point and since I had decided to take charge of the group and depose Dr Parrish's leadership, I wanted to know who they were.

I held up a hand. 'While Michael fiddles with the elevator and tries to get it to work, I think we would benefit from finding out who we all are. I'll start. I'm Amanda Harper. I'm a paranormal detective. Point to note: there is no such thing as the paranormal.' I pointed to a witch whose face was now a confused O. 'You next?' I suggested.

'Um, I'm Hazel, I'm a sister of the earth and one of the sistren of earth witches. The supernatural world surrounds and guides me.' She was presenting an argument against my statement, but I ignored her as I pointed to the woman next to her.

Patience butted in, 'Wait. Sistren? What the heck is that?'

Next to Hazel, the blonde witch who liked to show her legs said, 'It's like brethren, but for women. I'm Lily, by the way, another witch.'

The other witches were Narcissus, Rosemary and Violet. When I got to the end of them, I noticed something amiss. 'Where's Lord Hale?'

Everyone looked around.

Hazel said, 'He came along this bit of the corridor with me.'

Next to her, Rosemary said, 'He needed to tinkle, I think. Said he wouldn't be long.' I shook my head. He led us to the elevator which means he thought that was our way out. If he needed the bathroom then we were just about to access the rest of the house and find lots of them. Why would he sneak off now?

'Everything okay?' asked Big Ben.

Pursing my lips, I replied, 'I'm not sure. I don't entirely

trust our host anymore. I could say there is something strange going on, but that's so obvious as to be laughable. I want to see where he went.'

'Maybe he tried the stairs,' said Dr Parrish, appearing so close to me in the dark that it gave me a start.

'Stairs?' Big Ben and I said at once.

Knights

Just like any building, this one had stairs as a back-up to the elevator. It was the intended route out for the guests once they had solved the riddle in the library. Dr Parrish explained all this merrily as he led us through the dark passageways. I wanted to ask why he hadn't mentioned the stairs before and why we were not already leading the group that way now. I almost went back for them, but something intangible stopped me. I wanted to see what Lord Hale was doing, without him seeing us. In other words, I wanted to see his behaviour when he thought himself to be alone.

Dr Parrish led us through passageways, back past the exit from the library and around a corner. This time I had the lamp held by my knee to limit the amount of light it cast. I had a feeling Lord Hale was up to something, especially since we didn't find him around a convenient corner taking a tinkle. He chose to sneak off when the rest of us were distracted by the elevator, seizing his first chance to get away now that we were no longer trapped in the library.

When we reached the first junction, he went left and sent us all right. That was my guess anyway.

Dr Parrish was still jabbering on about planned additional levels of escape room they could yet employ but I spotted a light ahead and clamped a hand over his mouth. Squinting in the dark, Big Ben and Dr Parrish doing the same, I could make out what looked like a phone screen. It was jerking about, but as it was lifted into the air, I caught a glimpse of Lord Hale's face reflected in the light from the screen. I took my hand away from Dr Parrish's mouth, but he instantly drew in a breath to speak and I had to clamp it back in place to stop him.

Lord Hale was making hushed, but urgent and very angry threats. By keeping quiet we could hear him. 'Where the hell are they? They had better not have double crossed me. Why haven't they answered?' I wanted to know who he was referring to. 'I can't distract them for much longer, they must know that, how long do they think I can keep them down here?' He made a move like he was trying to squeeze the life out of his phone in frustration, swore loudly and hurried away from us.

As we moved to follow, Dr Parrish tripped, pitched forward and knocked the lamp from my hand. It hit the floor and broke, the paraffin inside spilling to ignite. It wouldn't be a problem on the stone floor; there was nothing combustible around to burn. However, if the noise it made hadn't been enough to give our presence away, the bright flames at our feet certainly were.

'Who's there?' called Lord Hale, failing to keep the fright from his voice.

'Where are you going, Lord Hale?' I called after him, my voice sufficient to make him run.

I started after him, instinct making me give chase like a

cat who has seen a rabbit. Dr Parrish ran too, catching up after only a stride or so. 'Why did he run?' he asked, befuddlement in his voice.

I shrugged, but realising he couldn't see that, I yelled between breaths, 'Let's ask him.'

'He's heading for the stairs,' Dr Parrish puffed, keeping up with me, but both older and less fit than me, he was starting to show the effects of his effort. I glanced back to see Big Ben still following close behind. Around the next dark corner there was light. Not a lot of it, but enough for it to emanate a glow as we neared. 'It widens ahead,' Dr Parrish managed. I got the impression he wanted to stop for a breather but there was no time for that.

'We've missed him,' shouted Big Ben. 'He's eighty years old. There's no way he could outrun us. He ducked in somewhere and we passed him.'

I put the brakes on. Why hadn't I thought of that? Skidding to a stop and taking a breath, Dr Parrish bent over double and gasped for air. He tried to speak, but couldn't get enough air in, so held up a finger to ask for a moment's grace and went back to trying to breathe.

We had come to a stop right at the corner where the glowing light shone. Dr Parrish was right about it opening up, the new passageway was four times as wide and had suits of armour lining each side. On the walls behind the armour were more weapons, pikes, swords, lances and more, each pinned in place by steel brackets and between them were burning torches, half a dozen of them on each side, throwing dancing light in every direction.

In the distance, beyond the knights in their armour, was a set of stairs. 'Perhaps we should just get the others and get out,' I suggested. It wasn't really a suggestion though; it was the thing we were going to do. Nothing else could be considered even remotely sensible.

I expected Big Ben to nod his agreement, but looking at me, his focus shifted to look beyond me to the stairs. 'Hey, there's Lord Hale,' he pointed and started moving. 'How on earth did he stay ahead of us?' He was right, the old man must have been hiding in a shadow when we got to the corner and was trying to sneak up the stairs now. I was also curious to hear how he had got there so fast but assumed there was a shorter route than the one we had taken. In the dark, I had lost sight of him several times.

Dr Parrish was in front of us both, waving an arm at the retreating lord as he called, 'Lord Hale! Lord Hale, where are you going? Your guests are still down here.' Then he glanced back at us with a shrug and a grin, 'I guess he is getting a little deaf. I hope I'm that sprightly at his age though.'

He was walking backwards to speak to us, so didn't see the first suit of armour move, but I did, and I saw that Dr Parrish had heard it. I gasped, unable to mask my shock as the knight stepped down from his podium and turned to face us with his sword raised.

'Don't worry,' said Dr Parrish with a chuckle. 'I had a hand in these actually. We only just had them installed. Damned expensive animatronics, but sure to give the guests a solid scare when we get to this point.' More of the knights were joining the first in the passageway to bar our path though Dr Parrish couldn't have been less concerned about them. 'At least it means the chaps are back in the control room. They get operated from there. I'll give them a shout and tell them to put the kettle on.' Dr Parrish reached into his jacket to get his radio, patted his pockets and made a glum face. 'I forgot; Lord Hale has my radio.'

Dr Parrish was surprised when the first one stuck him with a pike. He had just turned around with a plan to side-step the walking suits of armour and was too close to them to get out of the way when it thrust forward with its right arm.

I choked out a gasp of surprise myself, something I felt like I had been doing all evening, but Big Ben burst into action. As Dr Parrish fell backwards away from the knight, clutching his side and whimpering, the giant double-headed battle axe Ronald the dwarf had been wielding took the knight's head clean off. It sparked and fizzed as it fell backward, and that might have been that, but my large friend wasn't taking any chances. There were eight knights in total, goodness knows what they must have cost to make, but Big Ben reduced them to scrap in less than ten seconds, the giant axe whirling in fast circles from his right hand as he protected his injured left shoulder.

Dr Parrish was trying to say something. Cradled in my arms, his eyes were wide with a desperate need to speak but the pain from his wound kept him from forming the sentence until it was too late. 'I walked into the blade; it didn't attack me. They are just machines,' he managed finally, clearly upset that Big Ben had destroyed them.

'It looked like it took a swing to me,' I replied. Big Ben just looked pleased with himself. 'How long have you had that axe?' I asked.

'I picked it up after the thing killed Ronald. It felt like a wise addition to my outfit.'

Dr Parrish tried to sit up, winced against the pain but managed to snarl, 'You just trashed a million pounds worth of robotics, you oaf. We never even got to use them.'

Big Ben crouched to get close to Dr Parrish, and I thought for a moment he was going to take issue with being called an oaf again. He placed the axe on the floor though and pulled Dr Parrish's hands away from the abdominal wound. 'You have to be careful with stomach wounds. If it nicked your intestines, you'll be in trouble quickly. You need to let us look at it.' With a yank, Big Ben exposed Dr Parrish's midriff. On the opposite side to where one might expect to find an appendix scar, was a deep puncture wound. Blood leaked from it which was a good thing because it wasn't gushing; there are some big arteries in that area. 'I think it's okay,' he announced. 'We need to dress it, and it will need closing as soon as we can find something to do that with.'

'We need to fetch help,' I pointed out grimly. 'We have two dead and now two injured, plus Tempest is missing still. Whatever is going on, it isn't finished. Somebody activated the knights on purpose to stop us or slow us down.'

With a nod, Big Ben stood up, hefting the axe once more in his right hand. 'I'll see what I can find.' With that he went for the stairs and vanished up them, disappearing from sight as he climbed.

Dr Parrish was getting heavy. When he fell backward away from the knight as it stabbed him, I caught him, and he came to rest half on top of me as I lay him back on the floor. Now I needed to get up and it would be better for him to get him back to the library or something. 'Dr Parrish, I am going to try to get you up. I want you to relax and let me push you into a sitting position, okay?'

He nodded rather than speak but let himself go floppy so I could lever him upright. Now I was going to have to pull him off the floor by putting my arms under his and performing a dead lift. I licked my lips and geed myself up for the task, but there were footsteps coming back down the stairs already, the sound lifting my hope until I saw that it was Big Ben and he was by himself still.

Seeing my face, he held his arms out in defeat. 'There's a steel door at the top and it's locked. Had it been wood, I might have tried to beat my way through it with the axe.' The axe wasn't made for hacking through trees though, it was a weapon for slicing up people. Using it to cut through a wooden door would probably have just broken it.

The three of us looked at each other's faces in the flickering dim light: we were still stuck in the basement; all exits cut off.

To Trap a Demon

More questions were queuing in my head, chief of which now was why Lord Hale had run and why he then locked us down here. Dr Parrish couldn't explain it, he assured us, which wasn't very reassuring. The old man had snuck away and then ran when he saw us following. Clearly his intention was to evade us and leave us trapped in the basement. Why though?

I wasn't going to get an answer any time soon and I suspected I was going to have to work some of this out for myself if I wanted to get out of here.

Between us we got Dr Parrish back onto his feet, but I had to help him walk, his arm around my shoulder for support rather than Big Ben's because he is just too damned tall.

Trudging along the dark passage, Dr Parrish's weight making my back hurt, we all heard the low moan that always preceded the monster making an appearance. Big Ben said some colourful words as he looked about and hefted the axe. 'Come on little monster, come to Big Ben. I have a little present for you,' he sang like it was a nursery rhyme.

'It's in the basement somewhere,' winced Dr Parrish. 'It's hiding down here where it can pick us off. We need to stay together.'

'We need to get back to the others,' I agreed. 'Ben, come on.'

'Coming, dear,' he said as if we were husband and wife. 'I thought I saw something.'

I limped along with Dr Parrish draped over my shoulder to weigh me down. If the monster appeared, I was going to have to drop him so I could fight it. But suddenly Big Ben shouted, and I spun my head around to see it dart out of an alcove behind us.

'Come on then, beasty,' cooed Big Ben. 'Come and meet my friend, Mr Axe.'

I did my best to be gentle as I pushed Dr Parrish against a wall, but he cried out in pain anyway as he too turned to face the monster. In the dark, its glowing eyes were hideous and the blue glow from its mouth utterly fascinating. It stabbed at Big Ben with both front legs, Big Ben using the axe to defend himself. Sparks flew as the monster's claws hit the head of the axe.

It stabbed again, Big Ben parrying the blow but there wasn't much room to swing the axe in the tight corridor. I wanted to do something, but I had no weapon. That was until I spotted the house bricks on the floor. There were only two by the look of it, but I grabbed them, one in each hand. waited for my opening and threw the first as hard as I could.

It hit Big Ben in the back of his head.

I swore as he wobbled, his legs buckling beneath him and threw the second. This time I got the monster right in the face and it stumbled backward. Big Ben had gone down to one knee, so I snatched the axe from his hand but when I looked back up to face the monster, it was gone.

'What did you hit me with?' asked Big Ben.

'Um, a house brick,' I admitted unhappily.

'Yeah. That's what it felt like. Is it gone?'

'For now, I think. We shouldn't hang around though. I think it came for us because we were separated from the main group. We should get back to them.' It took a while to find our way back through the maze of basement passages, the sound of voices eventually reaching my ears just before the glow of light from their lamps came into view. Nearest us was the gaggle of witches, hanging around at the back of the small crowd because they could offer no help to the efforts with the elevator.

'Oh, what happened to Dr Parrish?' asked Lily as she noticed our approach and saw him shuffling along while holding his gut.

Big Ben said, 'Hey, babe. There was a minor incident with some knights in armour. I took care of it.' I rolled my eyes and was glad Patience hadn't been close enough to hear him setting up his next shag.

'We need to get him to a hospital. Dr Parrish, can you stand?' I asked, pushing him against a wall so it would keep him upright for a moment and give me a break.

He winced again as I slipped out from under his arm and allowed it to lower back to his side. 'Stand, yes. Run around and fight off a monster, probably not.'

Lily got in the way. 'I'm a paramedic,' she said, peering at Dr Parrish's face and starting to examine his wound.

'Really?' I asked.

She nodded, not taking her eyes from the patient. 'Being

an earth witch doesn't pay much. We all have proper jobs. Hazel is a schoolteacher, Rosemary a lawyer.'

Gina appeared out of the gloom. 'I found some more information on the monster. Further into that book there are some drawings. I believe they were created from eyewitness reports from when one of Lord Hale's ancestors was killed but Professor Wiseman cross referenced it against another book we found, and it might be that we can identify the beast.'

'Really?' Dr Parrish was instantly excited at the prospect.

'Yes!' Frank popped up, seemingly from nowhere with a giant grin on his face. 'There was something familiar about the circumstances of the curse. It has been bugging me since I got the invitation from Lord Hale and I curse myself that I didn't use my own resource material at the shop; it just didn't occur to me until ten minutes ago, but I have seen this before.'

'You know what this means?' Dr Parrish couldn't keep the excitement from his voice; he was almost bubbling over with it.

'Well, I don't,' said Tempest's mum, Mary, as she came to see what all the fuss was about. 'Michael thinks he can get the elevator working shortly. It's just a case of… no, I forgot what he said already. He was talking about electronics, which to me sounds like just as much rubbish as you lot talk.' I loved that she always said whatever she thought and never considered that she should hold back or consider other people's feelings.

It was Narcissus who provided the answer. 'We can summon and trap him,' she murmured. Despite his injury, Dr Parrish raised his hand for Frank to give him a high five, then winced when he got it.

'Trap him how?' I asked, wondering if I was about to regret the question.

Frank stepped by me, heading back the way we had come and away from the elevator and its prospect of escape. 'Back in the library, we have to find a way to complete the circle so we can use it.' He started making a mental list. 'We have to find a small amount of silver, some chalk to inscribe protective runes…'

'I have silver,' Narcissus admitted guiltily. 'When you asked us to look for it earlier, it didn't occur to me that my jewellery is silver.'

'Mine too,' said Lily, holding up half a dozen bangles. 'Will you need string?' she asked. 'I always keep some with me so I can make a dream catcher if I need one. They're such a versatile tool, don't you think?' Lily was a paramedic and looked like a normal person, but she really wasn't.

Hazel stepped into our circle, 'I have chalk.' She was holding a long stick of it between the finger of her right hand like a writing implement. 'I never go anywhere without chalk.'

Frank's eyes were lighting up as his shopping list got ticked off. 'We also need something sharp to make a cut and a cup or chalice of some kind to catch the blood we will use to invoke the cage.'

'We can find those things in the library,' suggested Dr Parrish with another wince. 'Do you still have your pocket watch?'

Frank held it up in response.

Gina asked a question, 'Can you banish it?' When Frank and the others looked her way, she said, 'Sorry, this isn't my area. I have never studied demons.'

'None of us have,' added Professor Pope, speaking for the academics.

'Which is why you need us,' grinned Frank, looking very much in his element. So far as I could make out, talking utter rubbish was his element.

'What else will we need?' asked Professor Wiseman.

Dr Parrish blew out a breath. 'We need the sigil of the demon.'

Gina started flicking pages of the book she held in an excited fashion. 'That's in this book, I think.'

'And we need a sacrifice,' Dr Parrish concluded solemnly.

'Say what now?' demanded Patience who apparently had been listening in. 'You crazy white folk can get up to all kinds of weird stuff if you want to, but I got to draw the line at human sacrifice.'

'Not human sacrifice, Patience,' Frank said quickly. 'It can be anything. Typically, a mouse or quite often a chicken because you can have it for dinner afterwards.'

Patience's eyes bugged almost out of her head. 'You got to be kidding me.'

'No, really. Chickens are often used for sacrifice…'

She held up a hand to his face. 'Stop. I'm not talking about the chicken getting used for sacrifice.' She poked him in the chest. 'I'm talking about you bringing up the subject of chicken for dinner in front of a hungry woman who didn't get any. I need something to eat right now. I'm so hungry I'm gonna start gnawing on my handbag soon.'

'Riiight,' drawled Frank.

'Anything else on the list?' asked Gina.

'Any chance we can get a women's volleyball team, a Victoria sponge, and a tub of lube?' asked Big Ben, sniggering to himself while everyone ignored him.

Or almost everyone, because Lily had a question for him. 'What's the Victoria sponge for?'

In the dark, he growled like a tiger. 'Maybe I'll show you.' Then I heard a sharp intake of air as Patience hit him somewhere south of his belt.

'Boy, how have you got any energy left to be messing with this skinny white girl?' Muttering, she left him behind as she went to check on progress back at the elevator.

With nothing left to discuss, Frank, Dr Parrish, Lily and the witches, plus Gina and the other academics were all making their way to the library. 'You're really going to try to summon and trap Lord Hale's Monster?' I asked with disbelief dripping from every word.

At the head of the group, Frank paused and turned, the lamp he held distorting his features to make him look gruesome. 'It's actually a really simple process.'

'Not without risk to the practitioner though,' Dr Parrish reminded him.

'Have you ever done this before?' asked Gina, suddenly sounding worried.

'I have been involved with summoning and trapping many, many demons as an honorary member of the Kent League of Demonologists,' Frank boasted in return.

'Yes, yes,' she parried his response, 'but have you ever been the one conducting the summoning?' She turned her gaze to take in Dr Parrish as well. 'Have either of you?'

Neither answered, making small, 'Um,' and 'Err,' noises instead and picking their fingernails absentmindedly.

There was no hiding the concern in her voice when Gina said, 'I ask because my only knowledge of this practice comes from reading books, most of them written long ago before the practice died out. It died out, so far as I can perceive, because the practitioners kept getting themselves killed or dragged to hell, or, in several cases that I read, decapitated.'

Dr Parrish gulped. 'Yes, well, we have all the tools we need and it's not as if we are boozy students on a Saturday night with nothing better to do. We are going to get killed by the monster unless we stop it.'

'It's a guy in a suit,' I pointed out.

'Yeah,' added Big Ben. 'Just get him back here so I can cut off his arms,' he said with a swish of the axe, 'and then maybe we can go home.'

'What I saw wasn't a man in a suit,' argued Lily, though she took the opportunity to move closer to Big Ben's protective presence.

Dr Parrish shook his head. 'I don't think it was either. I saw Brian move about in the suit we made for him. I thought it was based on Lord Hale's imagination, but I guess he was drawing on memory from books his father, grandfather and other family members had shown him. It wasn't Brian that killed Ronald. It was the demon in that book.' He jerked a thumb at the thick tome Gina held.

'Yes, Quenti...'

'Shhh, never say his name outside of a protective circle,' snapped Frank as Lily, Narcissus, Dr Parrish and others all said much the same thing with equal insistence. More gently, Frank said, 'Come on. We have work to do.'

Only when the group started on their way back toward the library did Gina notice the thing that was missing. 'Wait a second. Where's Lord Hale?'

'He ran away,' I told her.

'He ran... wait, he's eighty years old.'

Big Ben laughed. 'Yes, and he outran the lot of us. Ducked down a passageway, set some mental killer robot knights on us and ran up some stairs to escape.'

Gina couldn't look more confused now if she tried. She wasn't the only one, but then Big Ben's explanation of events hadn't been brimming with well-considered detail. 'Robot... what? Stairs?'

'He locked a steel door at the top of the stairs, before you question if we could follow him and escape that way.'

Frank was frowning. 'Why would he run anyway? Why would he leave us here?'

It was a great question.

Criminal Behaviour

SUNDAY, DECEMBER 11TH 0114HRS

As they made their way back to the junction and turned left to head back to the library, my feet twitched with indecision. I couldn't decide where my priority should be. Escape ought to be number one on the list, but I was beginning to feel that escape was going to prove harder yet than it already had been. Our incarceration was deliberate, that much I was certain of. What I couldn't work out was what Lord Hale could gain by bringing us here just to lock us up.

Tempest's dad was still on his hands and knees fiddling with the controls for the elevator; trying to get power to it I assumed. Just in front of his face, the panel containing the call buttons hung open, exposing wires both inside the panel and hanging out where they connected to the button.

He explained what he was doing when he saw me approach. Not that I understood much of what he said other than the bit about there always being a feed even when the power was off, so all he had to do was find it, expose it and reconnect it to the feed to the motor. Then he could get the elevator's doors open. Apparently, it was already on our floor.

'Can't we just force the doors open?' asked Big Ben, happily volunteering for the task, no doubt.

Tempest's dad didn't look up from what he was doing when he answered, 'We could. But then all we have is a big box to get in and still no power to send it anywhere. What would be the point?'

Big Ben conceded with a grunt.

Letting him get on with the job, I joined Patience where she leaned against a wall looking bored a few feet away. 'I think there's a major bust here, if we can just figure out what is going on.'

'A major bust?' she echoed, suddenly interested. My good friend Patience wasn't much of a cop. She didn't have enough interest to ever be a detective. She would have been better suited to community work where she got to help abused women or offer help in some other way because it was a subject she had genuine passion for. Being a cop was better paid though so she stuck at it and had her eyes set on the prize of a proper pension when they finally kicked her out. Recently though, and largely with my help, she had performed several high-profile arrests, swooping in as I finished a case to arrest the criminals and take them into custody. It had earned her the attention of the chief constable for Kent, a large county with a lot of police in it. I heard she was in line for a major accolade when the next round of awards were announced. Of course, her boss, Chief Inspector Quinn, had claimed most of the praise, his own self-interest outweighing the need to do the right thing and acknowledge his subordinates' efforts. This might be another chance to get attention for herself though and in an environment where

Quinn couldn't claim to have any involvement or influence.

Keeping my voice quiet, I whispered, 'I think Lord Hale is up to something. Actually, I don't think we have even met Lord Hale yet.'

'Say what, girl. Who do you think that old man is then?'

'Think about it. He's eighty years old but he ran away from me faster than I could go to catch him. That's not right. There's something off about him, and I don't just mean his behaviour since we found Kevin's body. Did you notice he had a trace of make-up on his collar which looked like foundation?'

'Well, the makeup probably came from that 'ho, Lily. She likes to throw herself at men. I tell you; I see her look at Big Ben again, I'm gonna...'

'Patience,' I hissed to drag her back to the present. 'Whether it was Lord Hale or not. Whether he is actually eighty years old or not, he is up to something.' Finally, I had her attention. 'He stayed in role perfectly, pretending the monster was real.'

'I thought the crazy folk decided it was real and were off to trap it?' she questioned, now sounding confused again.

'I think if we were actually facing a demon from hell that came with the express purpose of killing people, there would be a lot more of us dead by now.' She didn't look convinced, but I pressed on. 'He stayed in role, right up until he couldn't continue the ruse any longer. When I called him out on the clean floors and the lack of bat poop, he seemed genuinely mystified that we didn't know we were playing an elaborate game.'

'Right, yeah. So what?'

'So he dropped the pretence, but we were still trapped. He was content for us to be trapped as if his sole purpose was to keep us out of the way. He wants us trapped down here. All that changed when we found Kevin's body. His body language changed like it was a big shock.'

Patience argued, 'A dude died, and he couldn't have killed him because he was with us. I think it was a shock.'

I had to give her that one. 'You're right. But what I mean is, he no longer seemed content to sit around and be trapped in the basement. The monster reappeared, which I don't think he was expecting and whether it was Brian, another one of the actors, or someone else inside the suit, Lord Hale was shocked when it killed Ronald.'

She nodded. 'He was, wasn't he? But again, so what? We were all shocked.'

I was having difficulty explaining my line of thinking, failing to get her head attuned to what I thought I was seeing. 'Yes, we were, but his reaction was different. If we assume that he knew there was a way out via the stairs he subsequently used, then he deliberately kept that information from us. He skulked about at the back of the pack until no one was paying attention and then snuck away. He ran when we followed and then locked us down here. Whatever it is that he is doing, he needs us tucked out of the way so he can do it.'

Patience stared straight at me. 'Let me get this straight. You think the old white dude is up to something in the house and that is why we are stuck down here, but you don't think he is responsible for the two murders?'

'Yes. I mean no. I mean exactly that,' I was stammering and not making myself clear. 'He's guilty of something criminal but he isn't the killer. I don't think he faked his shock at Kevin's death, and I think it was what propelled him to flee. Kevin dying changed something about his plan, forcing him to leave us behind and escape.'

Patience squeezed my hand. 'You know that's a bit thin, don't you? Sounds like a lot of guesses and not much knowledge.' Well, she had me there.

'Got it!' whooped Tempest's dad, rocking back on his knees and jumping to his feet. 'Ooh, goodness, I can't do that anymore,' he complained, rubbing his legs and his back as his energetic leap proved too much for his old bones. Making a show of being in pain, he nevertheless picked up the elevator controls which now had a glowing red light behind them and pressed the up button.

The doors swished open, the light inside harsh in the gloom our eyes were adjusted to, but it did a really good job of showing us the crumpled body on the elevator floor.

Closing the Circle

SUNDAY, DECEMBER 11TH 0131HRS

'Oh wow,' said Patience, capturing nicely what everyone else was thinking. Tempest's mother crossed herself again.

When the door swished open to reveal the body on the floor, my heart had stopped for a moment as my paranoid brain told me it was going to be Tempest's face that I saw. It wasn't though, it was someone else. I grimaced at the task but got on my knees to examine him even though I really didn't want to. It struck me as ironic that now I had quit the police, I saw dead bodies far, far more regularly than I ever had before.

The man was big and when I say big, I mean like Big Ben big. Crumpled on the floor it was hard to estimate his height, but it was well over six feet, and he was very blocky. I patted for a wallet, found one and opened it to find the name I expected to see.

'It's Brian Carruthers,' I announced.

'The man who's supposed to be in the monster suit?' Mary asked.

I nodded. 'That's the one.'

'So who is in the monster suit?' asked Patience.

I had no answer for her. I carried on looking at the body. Brian was staring sightlessly out of the elevator, one hand covering his chest as if to protect it and the other lying limply next to him. There was no sign of violence. If it wasn't for his open eyes, I might have assumed he had gone to sleep. He was quite dead though, his skin cold to the touch and no trace of a pulse to be had. I performed a cursory check, Patience bustling into the car to help me. When we got to his neck, we found the tell-tale signs of strangulation. We had both seen these on women who survived domestic abuse, so we were sure what we were looking at.

'What do you think?' I asked Patience.

She tilted her head slightly as she considered her answer. 'I think he was killed by the monster. Or, at least by whoever is now in the monster suit because I prefer the idea that there is a person inside it than the monster is real.'

I wriggled my lips around a little in thought. 'The coroners will confirm it. We should get the others and get back to the surface. Maybe there we will find some answers.' I stood up, turning around to find Tempest's dad holding out his dinner jacket. I didn't get it for a second, but he was offering it so I could drape it over Brian's body. No one would want to ride the elevator with his sightless eyes staring at their bum.

With it in place, I touched Michael's arm in thanks. 'I'll be right back. Don't go up without us; we have no idea what might be happening up there.'

'Super,' grumbled Mary. 'Just the confidence boost I hoped for. Now we can escape here and get killed by someone up there.'

With her moaning whine fading behind me, Patience

and I made our way back to the library. I asked Big Ben to stay with them, just in case because whatever else I believed, I was certain there was a killer loose.

'How's your phone battery?' Patience asked, traipsing along behind me in the dark, both of us relying on my torch to see.

'Four percent and fading fast. Ah, make that three percent.' We both knew we needed to get to the surface soon or risk the entire group running out of light.

Frank's voice cut through the quiet as we approached the library, stepping around Kevin's body where he too lay with a jacket over him. 'How's the circle looking?' he asked someone just as we came into the room.

The library was a hive of activity, everyone doing something except Dr Parrish, who, in deference to his injury, was sitting on the table which they had lowered back down to floor level. The books which had been boosting it into the air were now stacked neatly on top, the neatness the result of the task being performed by academics no doubt. Dr Parrish, I noticed, wasn't looking very good. He was upright when he probably ought to be lying flat with his legs elevated and his wound still wasn't dressed. Dressing it wouldn't do much to stem the outflow of blood slowly leaking from his abdomen, but it would help.

Lily and Narcissus were crouched on the floor, doing something to the circle with their backs to us. Before I could ask Dr Parrish how he felt, Narcissus swung her head to answer Frank's question. 'It might hold. That's the best I can offer. We really need a crucible to melt the silver so all we can do is stuff it in as hard as we can and hope it holds. It will connect the circle but I don't know if we need to disguise it so the demon cannot spot the weak point.'

Dr Parrish winced as he tried to see what they were

talking about. 'You know what happens if the circle breaks, don't you?'

'I don't,' said Gina.

Frank pulled a face. 'Well, if it breaks after we call the demon but before we trap it, we will find ourselves trapped in a tight space with an enraged creature from hell who would like nothing better on his toast for supper than our kidneys.'

'Whoa, that's gross,' Patience complained while making a gagging noise. 'You are one nasty little man.'

Frank did a good job of painting the picture, but they could dispense with all this nonsense now. 'We got the elevator working,' I announced. 'We can get to the surface now and get out of the house. I'm sure that's welcome news for everyone.' Eleven sets of eyes looked back at me, none of the faces attached to them reciprocating my smile.

'We're nearly ready,' said Professor Wiseman. 'Can you wait a few minutes?' My mouth fell open. Was he kidding me?

'Actually, I have some bad news.' The latest announcement came from Tempest's dad as he filed into the room with his wife and Big Ben. 'The elevator operates with a key code. Probably four digits but I don't know. Without that, it doesn't matter what I do to the electrics, it isn't going anywhere.'

Now I remembered watching Travis put a code into a keypad when we first boarded it. Yet again, we were defeated, stuck in the basement with no way out.

Big Ben asked, 'How about I go through the access panel in the top of the elevator and climb up the cable to the next level?'

'Are you Bruce Willis now?' asked Patience. Then she cast her eyes to Tempest's dad. 'Would that work?'

'Doubtful,' he replied. 'Elevator cables are actually quite greasy. Two movement things running over each other constantly, a bit of grease is necessary.'

I filed that away for future reference. And turned to face the ailing man at the table. 'Dr Parrish, you must know the code for the elevator.'

'Yes, I… I, um.' He looked at me and I could see he was about to faint before he did, his hand slipping along the table as he lost consciousness and folded into himself. I couldn't get to him in time, and neither could anyone else, the wounded fool refusing aid until his condition worsened. Now his blood loss was at the point where he was out cold. We wouldn't get him back either, not without medical treatment. This was bad, the level of urgency just went up a notch. I tried to revive him so we could get the code at least, but he was unconscious; his pallor and thready pulse telling me we weren't about to hear the elevator code from him.

'We have to get him to the surface,' I said, my voice unwavering in case someone felt like arguing.

Frank looked about. 'No one else has the code for the elevator.' Patience came to her knees next to me and started rummaging through Dr Parrish's pockets. 'What are you doing?' Frank asked.

Patience flipped her eyes up at him. 'I'm searching for his Starbucks loyalty card.' Lily gasped and Frank drew in a breath to argue, but she got there first. 'I'm looking for his phone and wallet, dummies. I can never remember all the codes in my life, so I keep them hidden on my phone. This one's twenty years older than me, so he might have them on a note in his wallet but if he has the code for the elevator written down, I bet we can find it.' Triumphantly she produced his phone from an inner jacket pocket and then routed around under his butt until her hand reappeared with a wallet. With a quiet, 'Ta-dah!' she tossed the wallet in the air, so I had to catch it while she started fiddling with his phone. 'Fingerprint lock,' she explained as she grabbed his hand to open the screen.

'I still think we have to try to capture the monster,' said Frank to a chorus of agreement and approval from the witches and the academics. 'We can all fit inside the circle; it's big enough. The demon trap is set, we have a beetle to use as a sacrifice, so we are ready to go. All that remains is to invoke the sigil and call his name.'

I wasn't ready to move yet, the contents of the wallet failing to yield any codes jotted on a piece of paper, so I waved a disinterested hand in his direction so he could get on with whatever silliness he proposed. While he did that, I closed the wallet and peered over Patience's arm to see the phone. 'Anything?'

'Not yet. His notes app is empty. I guess he hasn't discovered it yet.'

'Ready?' called Frank.

'Huh?' I looked up. Patience and I were sitting in the middle of the circle and everyone else was around us, even Tempest's parents and Big Ben. Frank was on top of the table, bare chested to show a weird symbol drawn on his chest in what appeared to be red lipstick. The same symbol was on his back I saw when he spun in place.

'Hold on, Frank,' I started to say but he was in full flow now, his eyes closed as he began shouting incantations.

'Daemon Quentinaxis obsecro te exibunt Invoco te typicus.' Was that latin? 'Quentinaxis Daemonis, infernum immolo tua mutare. Accipe sacrificium transiens.' Narcissus crushed something in a bowl. I guessed it was the beetle meeting his maker. 'Daemon Quentinaxis Quaero apparueris mihi.' This time Hazel stabbed Frank's outstretched thumb and caught the drops of blood in the same bowl in which the beetle breathed its last.

Nothing happened.

Frank opened one eye and looked about. I tried not to smirk, but Big Ben's shoulders were shaking in his attempt to keep his laughter under control. Frank opened his other eye. 'Maybe I did something wrong?'

Gina shrugged at him.

He pushed the flicker of annoyance from his face. 'Let's reset and try again. Have you still got the second beetle, Narcissus?'

Narcissus crossed the room to a drawer set into the shelves, opened it and scooped out a beetle with a very short life expectancy. Frank waved his arms with a flourish, waited for Narcissus to get back inside the circle, checked around to make sure everyone was safely inside the silver ring and tried again.

He got the same result.

'Are we done now?' asked Big Ben. 'Not that I didn't enjoy that. It was quite the show. With some special effects, you could make some money, I'll bet.'

Frank ignored him, choosing to address those who believed in what he was doing instead. 'Sorry, folks. Maybe I had the sigil wrong, maybe the name listed in the book isn't right.'

'Maybe you're all mental,' Big Ben said just about loud enough for them to hear.

I waved for him to be quiet; his comments were just sewing disharmony and I needed everyone to band together because I had an idea. I clicked my finger a few times to get their attention, when that didn't work, I made to clap my hands, but Patience stuck two fingers on top of her tongue and blew a whistle that almost burst my eardrums.

Now that she had their attention, she said, 'Amanda wants to say something. Listen up because it will be better than anything the fairy folk have to say.' She was staring at Frank when she said fairy folk, making sure he knew to keep quiet too.

Now that I was on the spot, I had to say something worthwhile. Fortunately, a plan was forming. 'Look, we all think the monster is going to come back, right?' I got a chorus of nods and yesses, all of them curious to see where I was planning to go with my question. 'Whatever it is,' I glanced at Patience and Big Ben, imploring them to keep quiet, 'it is manifesting physically. Maybe the reason your demon trap didn't work is because it isn't a demon.' Frank turned out his bottom lip to show he liked the idea because it meant he hadn't failed. 'I propose we create a real trap and lure it in. If it is a man in a suit, which I am pretty sure it is, then we can unmask him and maybe get some answers. How does that sound?'

Demon Trap

I think it was that no one had any other plan at all, let alone a better plan, that convinced them to concede to mine. Mine was simple enough; we were going to show the monster what he wanted and lure him into the trap with our own bodies. I swear I had seen the same thing done on multiple episodes of Scooby-Doo as a kid and once that thought crept into my head, I couldn't get the music from the show to stop playing. As I explained what I wanted to build and how we were going to force him into the trap, I was waiting for someone to offer me a Scooby snack.

No one else was on my wavelength though, all of them paying attention and asking questions as I drew out my plan on the surface of the table using a piece of chalk. When I finished, I drew a stick figure of the demon in the trap and a speech bubble with the words, 'Oh no! They caught me,' in it.

Everyone stared at it. Patience said, 'Hmmm.'

'Come on, let me have it,' I demanded, knowing she would have some quip to throw at me.

'I think it will work,' she replied.

'Really?' I was waiting for her punchline.

'Yeah. It's the dumbest plan I ever saw, but then I figure the guy in the monster suit must be pretty dumb, so he'll probably fall for it. Let's get to work.'

As the group split and started getting on with tasks, I checked on Dr Parrish again. 'How's he doing?' I asked.

Lily had taken it upon herself to care for him; none of us wanted to get on with things and come back to check on him only to discover he was dead. He wasn't though. She had dressed the wound, something he insisted wasn't necessary earlier when she first offered, and the blood had mostly stopped leaking out. It could still be leaking inward though there was nothing we could do about that. No matter what, we had to get him out of the basement and into the hands of some paramedics, or he would bleed to death.

Setting up the trap took less than fifteen minutes. When it was done, we all regrouped by the trap itself.

'Explain this to me again,' said Frank, eyeing the contraption dubiously.

'The library is our safe point, right? No one can get in unless they come in through the ceiling and with the mechanism that opened the original entrance broken,' everyone glanced at Big Ben, 'we can be sure no one is coming in through there so the only way out of that room is through the tunnel that the monster killed Ronald in. The monster is still down here somewhere moving about and waiting to pick us off, but it hasn't shown its face for a while because we haven't split up. Now we go out in twos, being super vigilant until one of us draws the monster out. We let it chase us - we are faster because the killer is wearing a heavy and cumbersome suit, and we lead it back to the tunnel that leads to the library. You, Frank, will be in the crawl space again, waiting for the monster to pass under you, at which point you will swing down and close the door, sealing the monster inside. It will then be trapped in just the library and the passageway leading to it. At this point the killer is still armed and not only dangerous but quite willing to kill so then we have to catch it.'

'That's where I come in,' said Big Ben, treating the situation seriously for once. 'Using grease from the elevator cable, the floor just inside the library will be super slippery. Whoever is being chased, needs to remember to jump it or they might get skewered by our mad monster when he catches up to them. They need to jump it and then get behind the table which will be turned on its side to form a barrier. Bookcases, objects and other things are arranged all along each side to create a funnel. The monster will have to go over the table, unable to see what is on the other side until too late. It lands in the big chest,' unable to help himself, he grinned at me when he said, "big chest," 'and we throw the net you made from the dream catcher string over him so he gets tangled.'

Looking at everyone, one at a time to make eye contact, I asked, 'Any questions?'

There were none so we split up, Tempest's parents heading back to the library where they ought to be safe, the elder academics with their beards going with them. Big Ben helped Frank to clamber up into the crawlspace, backing in so he could see out but would otherwise be invisible. The rest of us split into pairs. Patience with Gina, Big Ben with me, the witches in two twos because Lily stayed with Dr Parrish, and we all went in different directions.

Now we had to endure the least predictable part of the plan, where the monster would show up and who he would chase. Was he even down here still? I had to wonder about that because we hadn't seen him for a while and if his target, his true target for whatever reason, was Lord Hale, then did he know Lord Hale was no longer down here with us? Maybe he did and we were setting a trap for a monster who had already taken himself upstairs.

It was my bet that he was trapped down here as well. Maybe he had been using the stairs, but we hadn't seen him since Lord Hale locked the door at the top so if there were no other exits, then he was in here with us. It was a spooky thought.

Just at that moment, my phone crapped out and the light from it died. Big Ben turned his on. Thankful that we had some light, I asked, 'How much battery have you got?'

He peered at his screen. 'Not much.' His answer didn't tell me a lot, but it didn't really matter what percentage power it had left. Sooner or later we were going to be stuck below ground with no light source of any kind and no phone signal. We had no way of getting a message out and thus little chance we would be rescued any time soon. That was bad news for all of us. Especially Dr Parrish who would not be afforded the luxury of starving to death if we didn't deal with his abdominal wound soon.

My dilemma now was that I needed the monster to get on and spring his next attack in the hope that we could capture him and force him to give us the code for the elevator to enable our escape, but I was also terrified of getting attacked in the dark by a gruesome creature. I knew it was just a man in a costume. Well, ninety nine percent certain, but he had already killed Ronald for sure, probably killed Kevin and Brian as well, and injured Big Ben.

'How's the shoulder?' I asked, suddenly remembering his wound.

A loud crashing noise stopped him from answering. In

the dark, we looked at each other for a split second. Then as one, we yelled, 'The library!' and started running.

I couldn't be certain, but I was willing to bet the monster had avoided the bait and gone straight for the library; the crash we just heard, its entry through the ceiling. Running down the dark passageways, neither Big Ben nor I heard or saw Gina and Patience as they came at us from a right angle. All four of us collided in a tangle of limbs and I got someone's elbow to my lips as we all fought to get back to our feet. Ignoring the taste of blood, I got running again, wondering what I must now look like compared with the neat, tidy, ballgown-clad version of myself that had arrived at dinner a few hours ago.

Frank called something to me as I ran beneath his hidey-hole, but I didn't hear what it was. Ahead I could hear Tempest's father shouting and Mary wailing and cursing. I went around the bend, bouncing off the wall in the passageway in my haste to get to the library, and there, before me, was the monster, its arms raised above its head to reveal terrible talons where its hands should be. The limbs were too long though, obviously fake to my mind, but that was an insignificant factor because it was about to kill Tempest's dad.

'Hey!' I screamed, a banshee war cry coming from my lips as I charged into the room. I forgot the grease though, my front foot finding it and spilling me. Out of control as I slid, I could see I was going to hit the table and there was nothing I could do about it. I slammed into it with my whole body, shunting it back two feet so it hit the monster.

In surprise or shock, the man in the suit danced back in case the table toppled on his feet, but I wasn't getting up to deal with him or defend anyone. Thankfully, I didn't have to as my back up arrived in the form of Patience Woods:

police officer, angry black woman, and now axe wielding maniac.

I guess Big Ben didn't get up fast enough because as I saw her running toward me, Gina was behind her but there was no sign of the giant, muscular man; sisters were doing it for themselves today.

Unfortunately, Patience had also forgotten about the grease, and I couldn't get my brain working fast enough to shout a warning. She lost control just as I had, her front foot hitting the grease, but she pitched forward rather than skid and the motion sent her arms pinwheeling, the axe flying from her hand to zoom over my head. I didn't see the strike, tucked behind the table as I was, but I heard it and the crash that followed.

Feeling pain just about everywhere and still tasting blood from my lips, I grasped the top edge of the upturned table and peered gingerly over it. Hope for the best, plan for the worst and when none of that works, get your BFF to kill a monster with an axe.

The Guest in the Elevator

Mercifully, despite my initial concern, the axe she threw hadn't taken the monster's head off. It hadn't done much damage at all. Through blind luck it was the eye, the bit of the handle that poked through the top, that struck him. Frank, Big Ben and the witches all thundered down the passageway toward us, but met with Gina, who spread her arms and legs to ward them off and prevent a further pile up on the greased floor.

Being careful where I planted my greasy feet and using my trashed dress to clean the worst of it from them, I climbed over the table to safety. Patience got to her feet as well, though as I turned around to join Tempest's dad, I heard her shout an expletive. It was followed by a thump as she landed back on her arse, which was in turn followed by a tirade of expletives as she swore revenge on anything that ever got in her way for the rest of all time to come.

There was no sign of movement from Lord Hale's monster, save for the gentle rise and fall of its chest. Now that we could get close, I could see how fake it looked. The dark fur covering its body was polyester fibre and I could see the seam beneath its arm. The arms of the person inside the suit ended where the elbows of the monster suit bent so the wearer had to be gripping the forearm using a handle hidden inside. That would give it thrusting power for the knives on its hands which were shaped to look like talons but had probably never been designed for someone to sharpen.

'Be careful, Michael,' warned Mary, her sudden voice in the tense silence of the room enough to make her husband physically jump. With one hand on his chest and the other supporting his weight as he leaned against a bookcase, he shot a look back at her.

'Why would I worry about him when you can kill me with a word?' he asked. She poked her tongue out at him.

Remembering a line from Scooby-Doo, I stifled a grin before it got to my face and said, 'Let's get his mask off and see who it is.' I glanced around but nobody picked up on my reference. Disappointed, I crossed the remaining few yards and grabbed the head. 'Ben, can you give us a hand.' I didn't need Big Ben, anyone could help me, but I wanted the guy out of this suit before he could come around and stab someone; Big Ben was undoubtedly the strongest of everyone present.

With Big Ben holding the suit's forearms, Michael and I wrenched the head piece free. It was attached by some electrics, necessary to make the eyes glow, but it came free and we saw the killer for the first time.

I recognised him instantly. When we arrived, he helped us carry our bags in along with Matthew, the man hunk Patience drooled over. Neither had spoken, but Matthew's eyes had given the impression there was something going on behind them, this guy's hadn't. He was a hulking brute of a man, which given the size of the monster, should have been obvious. His head, the only bit we could see at the moment, was like a lump of granite, his close-cropped hair revealing scars on his scalp, and his nose was a flattened mess, partly because that was where the axe had hit him. It struck me that he was the same size as Brian Carruthers, the dead guy in the elevator, which made sense because it was supposed to be Brian in the suit, not this guy. I couldn't remember his name though I knew Travis had introduced him earlier.

Convinced he would soon come around and hoping he would so we could quiz him, I got Michael to help me to sit him up. Ten minutes later, he was out of the suit and tied to a table leg with his hands and feet tied separately. Manoeuvring him had taken six people, because he weighed so much. His entire body was muscle, not like a body builder, more like a person that spent their working life lifting heavy things – basically he reminded me of a forklift truck.

He was starting to come around, his head twitching as if asleep and his eyelids fluttering. I gave his face a tap.

'Don't tickle him,' growled Big Ben. 'Punch him in his ugly mouth.' I shot him a disparaging look. 'Hey, he cut a hole in me. There's some score to even.'

I tapped his face again, slightly harder this time, but in no way violent. I had too much police training in me to start abusing prisoners. His eyes snapped open, saw me and he jerked his whole body as he tried to get up. The bindings held, trapping him in place. 'Hello, I'm Amanda. Can we start by doing introductions?' I kept my tone polite and engaging, I needed answers.

'Where's Lord Hale?' he growled back at me, looking all around the thirteen faces looking at him. 'I want him, and I want that git, Parrish. Give me them and the rest of you can go free. They have to die though.'

'Why?' I asked, it was a simple question, though not the one I intended to ask first.

He stopped looking about and focused on me. 'You don't need to know why. Just give them to me and I'll let you live.' Back during my time in the police, I had to interview a lot of people. Some of them were innocent, caught up by being in the wrong place at the wrong time but a lot of them were hardened criminals, like this guy, and I had never been any good at convincing them to reveal what I wanted to know.

I tried a new tactic. 'Lord Hale escaped. You knocked out the power, didn't you? You wanted us down here so you could kill your targets, but you forgot to lock the stairs, and he escaped through them. Now you are trapped down here just like us.' I was guessing some of it, assuming he had accessed the basement via the stairs, but his eyes betrayed the truth of it. 'Tell us the code to the elevator and I promise we will leave you here. Maybe you escape the ropes, maybe you don't, you get nothing if you don't help us first.' He said nothing, glaring at me with angry eyes. Then he flexed his broad shoulders and tried to break the string holding him in place. I worried for a moment that he might be able to, but he gave up after a few seconds, veins standing out on his forehead from the effort. 'We need the code for the elevator. No one gets to go anywhere until you give us that.'

'I don't know it,' he snapped at me. 'I'm not deemed worthy enough to have it.'

This was better, now he was talking, and he just told us something. Now I had to use it to get more details. 'You're a footman here at the house, so what's your beef with Lord Hale and Dr Parrish?' He didn't reply, but he looked like he wanted to. 'They don't have any connections apart from their escape room / murder mystery business idea. What did they do to you?' Then it hit me: How would he know to dress as the monster? Better yet, how would he know to turn up tonight? 'They didn't give you the job as the monster, did they? Or did they give you the job and then fire you?' I waited a few seconds for him to answer, crouching in front of his face to make as much eye contact as possible.

Then, when I took a breath to ask the next question, he interrupted me. 'I was the right man for the job. They just refused to see it.'

'For the job as the monster?' I asked tentatively, not sure I had it right.

'I played stage and screen monsters. I've been in six episodes of Dr Who over five different seasons. They weren't going to find a better monster. So, they gave the role to that two-bit hack Brian.' Then he chuckled to himself. 'You should have seen his face when he found me in the suit. He thought the monster had really come to life. Not even the old man thinks the story is true but darken the lights, play the part well and everyone is terrified whether they want to be or not.'

My thoughts skipped to Tempest. He hadn't been afraid. He had been curious. The last time I saw him, he had blood coming from his head. That was hours ago, and I had no idea if he was alright or not. I forced down my emotions but because no one was talking, I think every single one of us heard the elevator's motor hum into life. It is a distinctive enough sound for me to not question what my ears believed I could hear.

I jumped to my feet, but I wasn't the only one moving; others were coming with me. I forgot the lump on the floor, abandoning him to see who was coming and if they were going to rescue us or present us with a new problem.

Jumping to get over the greasy bit of the floor, I paused to let Big Ben go into the passageway first; he still carried the axe in one meaty fist and would be the perfect person to receive our visitors no matter what their intentions.

We arrived at the elevator and only then did I realise my error. The sound we heard was the elevator moving. It had been on our floor; it wasn't now. Someone above had summoned it, so now it was travelling up to them. We were still trapped.

There was no sound in the passageway and most of the remaining dinner guests waited with bated breath to see what would happen next. We all heard someone get into the elevator. Just one person I thought. They paused once inside, possibly wondering what to do with Brian's body, which I decided had to be the case when we heard them drag his body from the car. It sounded like a difficult task. A moment later, the single set of footsteps returned but it was followed by another set. Then the elevator started moving again, coming our way for certain and I got ready to charge the occupant. Whoever it was, I was going to make sure we could secure our way out. Dr Parrish was alive but still unconscious and he needed help, so all I could think about was forcing our way back to the surface. From there we could break out of the house, find help, and find out what was going on. Our options weren't infinite but right now we had no options at all.

I almost felt sorry for the occupant of the elevator because whoever it was, they were about to get a nasty shock.

The car jerked to a halt and the motor stopped humming just before the doors slid open. I could feel my mouth all but snarling as I poised like a sprinter crossed with a wrestler, ready to pounce.

'Hello, Amanda,' said Tempest through the expanding gap in the door. 'Did I miss anything?'

I sobbed. It wasn't faked or forced; it was just what my body did in response to seeing him. I couldn't decide whether to laugh or cry or just wrap him up in a hug, but he was upright and alright and still looking great. His jacket was gone, much like Big Ben's and he had blood on his white shirt from the cut to his head. His bow tie was untied, the ends hanging loose from his collar, but he looked otherwise unscathed. Despite that, he was being partly held up by Lady Emily Pinkerton, who I now knew was called Anne Richman. I spotted her profile on Dr Parrish's Employable app. Another failed actor no doubt but one who was, hopefully, on our side.

Big Ben put the end of the axe's handle on the floor and leaned on it. 'Where have you been, slack bladder? Having a nice lie down? A cup of tea and biscuit?' He was teasing, equally glad to see his friend but the two men would never acknowledge any kind of brotherly feelings out loud.

The elevator doors tried to close, Big Ben's enormous foot stopping them. Tempest's dad pushed through to the front of the crowd now surrounding the elevator. 'How you doing, kid?'

'I have a concussion,' said Tempest with confidence. 'My eyes won't work right, and I am quite off balance but otherwise I am fine. I hit my head on a chunk of stone it would seem though I don't actually remember doing so.'

'We saw you,' I said, offering my hand to get him out of the elevator, then stopping myself. 'Do you have a code for this thing? How did you get it to move?'

'I have the code,' Anne said, speaking for the first time.

Tempest shook his head as if trying to clear it. 'Yes, Anne had the code. We found Brian Carruthers by the way.

He's supposed to be the monster. Someone strangled him, I think. He was in the elevator.'

'We found him too,' I said quietly.

A tear rolled down Anne's cheek. 'He was such a sweet man. We moved him and… well, I want to say he is comfortable now.' She trailed off, looking like she had more to say, but making no attempt to say it.

'Can we leave now, Tempest?' asked his mother. 'I have had a really crappy evening, and I want to go home.'

'Yes, about that,' he replied, trying to straighten himself up. 'We have a minor problem upstairs.'

Concussion, Injuries, and a Prisoner

SUNDAY, DECEMBER 11TH 0249HRS

'Hey guys! What's going on? Is everything okay?' Frank's voice echoed through to us from the library where he was undoubtedly shouting down the passageway to learn if we were all being murdered or not.

Professor Wiseman was nearest the passageway. 'It's Tempest and Anne. Nothing to worry about,' he shouted back.

'There's a whole lot of activity going on.' That was Tempest's big news. He was clearly concussed or something because he was slow putting his thoughts across.

Anne picked up his story. 'We had to wait ages for the coast to be clear so we could get down to you.'

Tempest added, 'Not that I was sure you were still down here, of course.' He looked around at everyone, all of us were staring at him and he seemed to be seeing us for the first time. 'You, ah… you all look a lot rougher than I expected. What did I miss?' he asked for a second time.

I felt sorry for him. Tempest had a naturally guilty conscience and always wanted to protect everyone, even when it was vastly impractical. There was no time for that though. 'Dr Parrish is injured, he's lost a lot of blood so whatever we are going to do, we need to do it soon, he just can't wait.'

He nodded in understanding. 'The only way we can do this is by bypassing the ground floor and heading to the upper floors. There are too many people on the ground floor, and they are busy.'

'Busy doing what?' asked his mother. 'Why can't we ask them for help?'

It was Anne who replied, 'They are up to something. I don't know what, but they are armed. We almost ran into them when I took Tempest back up to the surface to treat his headwound.'

I Interrupted her, 'Armed? Armed how?'

She pulled a face to express she wasn't sure what the right words were. 'They all have guns. Big black nasty ones.' This was not good news, but it did explain a few things. It also created several more questions. 'I'm not sure what they are doing,' she explained. 'Because too much snooping would have got us caught, or, at least, have increased the likelihood that we would get caught.'

Tempest spoke again, 'Lady Emily... oh, did you know she was an actress? Her name's not Emily at all.' Poor Tempest thought he was revealing a big secret. 'Her accent changed once we were away from everyone, that was my first hint.'

He was wandering off topic. 'Tempest, the people upstairs?' I reminded him.

'Hmmm?'

'I think perhaps we should get you sat down some-where.' I went into the elevator to move him to one side. His eyes didn't seem to be meeting in the middle, it was like he was drugged or drunk or something. Doing some mental math, I figured we could get everyone into the elevator, but it was going to be a struggle with Dr Parrish because he wouldn't be standing up.

'Oh,' said Anne suddenly. 'I just remembered. They kept saying the name Alexander. Lord Hale showed up and was shouting about it. He seemed very upset and wanted him found. Is he down here somewhere? He's one of Lord Hale's footmen.'

Bingo, I had the man's name. Not that it made a lot of difference. He was already in custody. Regardless, it was time to get moving. 'Ben, can you keep an eye on Tempest?'

'Don't you want a hand with Dr Parrish? Someone's got to carry him. I'm the obvious choice.' He wasn't bragging, he was just the biggest and strongest in the crowd. In almost any crowd for that matter.

'I've got him.' Tempest's dad moved in to keep an eye on his son, Mary just behind him and some of the witches started to shuffle into the elevator car. Anne, not part of the group until now and already being treated as an outsider, shuffled to the side to make room. I passed the academics as I headed back to the library where we left Lily, Narcissus, Patience, and Frank with Dr Parrish and the killer.

On my way in, I called out, 'Hey, Alexander.' The big man tied to the table snapped his head around upon hearing his name. He hadn't wanted to tell me his name, but now he knew that withholding it hadn't achieved anything. 'How's the patient?' I asked Lily.

Lily looked up. 'He's getting weaker. Is it really Tempest? Is he okay?'

'He's mostly okay. He had Anne with him.' Her face went quizzical. 'Lady Emily the vampire – her real name is Anne Richman. Anyway, he could do with some medical treatment too. The elevator is working so it's time to go.' Big Ben gently scooped the unconscious Dr Parrish into the air and started back to the door, edging around the greasy bit of the floor as he went. Lily and Narcissus followed, then Frank and Patience.

'What about me?' asked Alexander the murderer.

Patience paused. 'I read you your rights. You remain under arrest. I'll be back for you later. Until then, I left a light on for you.' That seemed to cover it. I felt sure he was safe enough though the lamp we left him was going to go out at some point and leave him in total darkness. Patience would come back later with a whole team of officers to escort the homicidal maniac out in cuffs. Attempting to do anything else now was pure folly.

As I started toward the door, something caught my eye and I stopped. 'Hey, Frank. Can you give me a hand with this?'

'Yeah, sure.' He had to come back a few yards to help me lift it. Not that it was heavy, just a little bulky. 'What do you want it for?'

I gave him a tight-lipped grin. 'I have a feeling it might come in handy.'

Control Room Raid

SUNDAY, DECEMBER 11TH 0313HRS

We bypassed the ground floor to ride the elevator to the first floor, where those nearest the doors, Lily and Frank, peered out carefully to check the coast was clear. They each gave a silent nod, their indication that we were safe to exit. There were a lot of us squeezed into a tight space, but I also think we felt safer that way because no one wanted to wait in the sub-basement. What if the elevator got called by someone else?

It didn't matter where we went from here, but our rooms weren't all that far away, so we headed there, reaching Mary and Michael's room first. Tempest was ambulant and coherent. Mostly. I wasn't content to involve him in whatever activities were to follow though, so once inside, I reversed him into a chair and made sure he was comfortable. Dr Parrish went onto the bed, Big Ben gently lowering him down before stepping away so Lily could check him again.

Mary pulled a bag onto the bed and started rummaging

in it. 'I have snacks,' she announced, producing a Tupperware tub full of cookies. 'Help yourself.' Seeing a stampede coming, she snagged two for herself and got out of the way.

Leaving them to it, I watched Lily, so I saw it when fear flashed across her face. I thought for a second that Dr Parrish was dead; that we had waited too long, but she found his pulse and breathed a sigh of relief. Patience leaned in close to her ear to ask a question quietly enough that no one else would hear it, nodded her head and stepped away.

She flashed her eyes at me and motioned across the room with her head. I followed. 'He's not going to make it,' Patience told me quietly. 'It's a fourth murder but you said it was a knight that stabbed him?'

'Yes, an animatronic one that came to life by itself. A load of them did.'

Patience gave me a single raised eyebrow. 'I doubt they came to life by themselves. Someone pressed a button somewhere which might not technically be murder, but it's something close to it.'

I thought about that. 'Anne said Lord Hale was giving orders to the men downstairs.'

'Do you think we can trust her?' Patience had a point. She hadn't been part of tonight's proceedings, and she could have caused Tempest's injury on purpose. We didn't know anything about her.

'Let's just keep a close eye on her. We should run through what we do know.' Patience and I distanced ourselves from the rest of the dinner guests by going over to the window. It was the coldest point in the room so no one else was there.

'What do we know?' asked Patience.

I chuckled darkly. 'Not much. We know… No, that's wrong. We believe that we were expected here for dinner tonight to be the test run for a fancy, swanky new escape room slash murder mystery event, but that part of the invitation got changed so we had no idea that it was all fake.'

Patience made notes on a pad she found by the bed. 'So someone messed with the invitation you received weeks ago which suggests this was all planned.'

'Meticulously planned,' I agreed. 'But Alexander the crazy killer in the monster suit turned up and killed the guy they hired for the role.'

Tempest's dad came towards us, causing us both to pause our conversation. 'Mind if I join you ladies?'

'Where's Mary?' I asked.

'Getting showered and changed. You know what she's like,' he said by way of explanation.

I didn't, though I was beginning to form a picture. 'We're just talking through what we might know before we try to do anything else.' He sat on the edge of the windowsill to listen. 'He also killed the magician.'

'Wizard,' Patience corrected me.

'Yes, wizard. Kevin something. He killed him and Ronald and wanted to kill Dr Parrish and Lord Hale for their part in not hiring him. He is most likely also responsible for killing Brian.'

'That's nuts,' said Tempest's dad.

I couldn't disagree. 'I don't think Alexander has anything to do with what is going on downstairs though. I think he caught Lord Hale by surprise. His whole attitude shifted when we found Kevin dead.'

'Yeah,' said Patience. 'It was as if he had a plan but now the plan was in question.'

'Didn't he escape right after that?' asked Michael. 'Like at the very first chance he got?'

'That's how it felt,' I replied. I was half listening to what Michael and Patience were saying and half trying to work the problem in my head. 'Who's in the tower?' I asked. Patience and Michael both shot me a look.

'What tower?' asked Patience.

I squeezed my eyes shut as if doing that would help the memory form. 'When we were approaching the house last night, there were lights on all across the ground floor but then no lights anywhere else except one right at the top of a tower.'

Patience remembered. 'You said it was really spooky and then scared the bejezzus out of me by saying someone just walked in front of the window.'

'That's right,' I nodded. 'So who's in the tower?' I couldn't come up with a reason to put someone in a tower unless they were: A. a princess, B. a prisoner. My money was on answer B.

Lightning flashed outside, making me jump. Michael jumped too but now he was staring out of the window, squinting at something in the grounds outside. 'Why would the catering vans still be here?'

I got up to join him, staring down into the murky black where I could see the sum total of absolutely nothing. Then lightning flashed again, and I saw them; half a dozen catering vans all lined up. It was gone midnight, the dinner for the party would have ended hours ago but the caterers were still here. If there were armed men downstairs doing something, then this was how they arrived.

Patience's voice was nervous when she spoke again. 'Amanda, what are we dealing with here? Armed men in the middle of nowhere, someone in a tower, multiple dead bodies and our host appears to be in on whatever is happening. If he is behind it and wanted us locked out of the way, why bother to bring us here? Are we supposed to be hostages?'

I frowned with doubt and worry. I just didn't know the answer. I could work out some of the bits of the puzzle but none of it made sense if Lord Hale was in on it. Why would he bring us here? I didn't think we were hostages; if that was always their intention, they made the task too complicated. They could have just snatched us and stashed us when we arrived. No. It was something else.

Lily caught my eye, 'He doesn't have much longer. All I need is an IV kit and some plasma. He's got a temperature coming too though; the wound probably did puncture his bowel. The longer we leave him, the less his chances of recovery are.'

From his chair across the room, Tempest said, 'There's a full first aid kit in the control room. It had a defibrillator, so it ought to have an IV kit with plasma too.'

Lily wasted no time. 'We have to get that kit now.' She was already on her feet and heading for the door.

'Whoa, whoa, whoa,' I got in front of her. 'You can't just go rushing off to get it. You don't even know where the control room is.'

Anne joined me. 'But I do. I can take you there,' she said quietly like she knew she ought to volunteer but really didn't want to.

This was good but we only had one axe as a weapon between the lot of us against men armed with assault rifles if Anne could be believed. I wasn't sure who I believed, truth be told. The one person whose word I would accept without question had his head scrambled. What I needed then, was to see it for myself. 'I have to go. I need to see what we are up against but our priority for now is to get the kit we need to help Dr Parrish.'

'I'm coming,' volunteered Big Ben as he moved toward the door. He rolled his shoulders and twisted his neck as if limbering up for a fight.

'If Lily is going, so am I,' announced Narcissus. They took to arguing about whether either of them should go, but Lily's training as a paramedic meant she had to go. Only she would know what kit Dr Parrish needed.

An explosion of swearing lit the room and drew our attention to Tempest's mother. She was on her knees in front of a cabinet. 'Everything alright, dear?' asked Michael.

She swung a vicious gaze his way. 'The Minibar. Is. Empty!' Around the room, dinner guests quickly hid the cans and miniature bottles they were holding.

Michael looked at me, his eyes imploring. 'I'm coming too.'

Less than a minute later, six of us slipped out of the room, Anne leading as we crept back to the elevator. It was still on our floor, which surprised me; I expected it to be more frequently used. We could hear the guys downstairs moving things about, talking at normal volume and clunking things around. It sounded like someone moving house, with boxes and bits of furniture going back and forth. I heard the sound of a pallet trolley being pumped up to drag a pallet somewhere and then the noise you get from one of those tape dispenser machines they use when they have lots of boxes to seal.

As I waited for the elevator doors to close, I spotted something on the wall opposite and stuck my hand between the doors before they could close. As they swung open again, I stepped out for a better look.

'What is it, Amanda?' asked Michael, keeping his voice to a whisper.

I pointed. 'See the shadow on the wall.' Everyone stared. 'There was something hanging there until recently.' Now that I looked, there were lots of shadows along the wall opposite the elevator and, when I stepped out to take a look, on the wall the elevator was set into as well. I wanted to investigate further, sensing that I was onto something, but Dr Parrish's needs were greater. I backed into the elevator and this time I let the doors close.

We all kept quiet, waiting for the car to arrive on basement level one where, Anna assured us, we would find the control room. We all got ready to leap out and attack, just in case there was a person or persons outside the doors when they opened.

The lights were on, but the basement looked abandoned; no sound or sign of life. It was as I had hoped but it still felt odd to get a lucky break tonight.

'It's to the right,' said Anne, pointing a finger but not leading the way. Playing the man as ever, Big Ben took off first, assuming the role of protector with his giant axe in his right hand still. Nothing opposed us, no one walked out of a room with their colleagues behind them to spoil our plan and we reached the control room after just a few strides.

Going in, the first aid kit and the defibrillator were easy to spot, the giant red cross above them a big giveaway. Anne cursed herself for not thinking about them when we first announced we had an injured man, but a quick check by Lily confirmed it contained everything she needed to keep him alive. She started to look around for a bag or a box to pack things into, but my attention was drawn to Narcissus, who was now sitting in one of the two big chairs in front of the wide expanse of monitor screens.

She was pressing buttons and checking screens, toggling between cameras and then reading labels on switches. 'Don't touch anything,' I warned, but she ignored me. As I crossed the room to quietly insist she desist before she pressed something that would identify us or draw attention where we did not want it, she turned to face me.

'I can operate this,' she announced. I stared at her for a moment. She raised an eyebrow. 'I'm a producer for the BBC. I've worked all kinds of jobs in the broadcasting industry. This is an old system, probably bought when a television studio upgraded theirs, it's easy to use though.' I looked down at the array of buttons, keyboards, switches and sliding things. I wouldn't even know how to turn it on. I could just as easily pilot the Millennium Falcon. I was about to tell her to forget it when she said, 'I can shut or open all the doors from here. And the windows. See this one?' she pointed. 'It says, *ground floor mist*.' I stared at the button. 'This one says, *ground floor trapdoors*.'

A jolt of realisation sparked in my head just as Michael joined us. 'We can turn the tables on them,' he murmured, echoing my thoughts.

'I can't find a box to put this stuff in,' wailed Lily from behind us.

'Just take it all?' I suggested, trying to stop myself from sounding like I was talking down to her.

'Oh, yeah. I hadn't thought of that,' she giggled to herself. 'Big Ben, can you carry this for me, it's very heavy.'

'Babe,' he growled at her in a playful tiger voice, 'I can carry you too.'

I slapped Narcissus on her shoulder. 'We need to get the

gear back to Dr Parrish. Do you want to stay here and familiarise yourself with the equipment?'

She nodded, her eyes never leaving the console. 'If you want to send an email to someone, I can do that from here too.'

This time I gasped. 'I don't have my phone with me. I need my contacts list. Ben,' I called as I turned around. 'Let's go. I need my phone, and I need Patience.'

We ran from the room this time, the first aid gear shared between us as we rushed to the elevator. The chance to make contact with the outside world meant we could contact the emergency services. Anne's report that the guys downstairs were armed meant I had to warn the police as well and have them turn up first with an armed response unit. We didn't know what they were doing, though the missing artwork gave me a pretty big clue. Why would Lord Hale be stealing his own art though? If this was an insurance fraud or a way to make money, then why invest so much in the escape room plan? Or had he overstretched and was now scrambling for any way he could find to pay off debts or complete the project.

Running through scenarios in my head, I found myself stuck in a cycle. I had to get help here quickly to save Dr Parrish. The plasma and drugs from the first aid kit would stabilise him but if his intestines were punctured, he was going to die without treatment. As I understood it, every minute counted. So we had to rush to get the police and medics here, but the house made for an excellent fortified position from which to defend. The thieves, if that was what they were, could use their weapons to keep the police at bay for hours, maybe even days. Worse yet, if I brought emergency services here in my attempt to save Dr Parrish, I invited the death of former fellow police officers as they exposed themselves to hostile fire.

I could only come to one conclusion about what course of action I needed to follow. I didn't get to follow that line of thought though because the elevator arrived on the first floor and as the doors swished open my heart sunk.

'Hello again, Miss Harper,' said Lord Hale. His bony arms were folded in front of his chest and a dozen armed men were pointing weapons in our faces.

Busted

SUNDAY, DECEMBER 11TH 0346HRS

'Put the axe down,' growled the nearest armed man, a short fellow with a Heckler and Koch MP5. He wore caterer's clothes, the emblem on his right breast matching that of the vans outside. Each of the men looked to have put in a hard day's work, the uniforms were smudged with dirt and grime and they were visibly sweating from the effort of moving and carrying.

'David? Derek?' Anne had taken a step forward until the guns all twitched in her direction. 'Guys, what are you doing with these men?'

'Shuddup,' one of them growled in response. She did, closing her mouth but continuing to stare. I would confirm it later, but they had to be the David and Derek from the control room. Now that I looked closer, one of them looked familiar – he was Mortimer Crouch, the paranormal detective that the monster snatched at the start of the evening. It proved to me that whatever they were up to had been in planning for some time because he was a mole they hired some time ago.

Ignoring them, the short man repeated his instruction, 'I said; put it down. I will not tell you again.' There was no trace of nervousness in the man's voice, he wasn't new to this. His steel blue eyes stared at Big Ben, looking up inevitably and looking unhappy about the height difference. His buzz-cut hair and lean shape suggested military. Whoever he was, he wasn't making idle threats.

Slowly, and without breaking eye contact, Big Ben lowered the axe to the floor. The rest of us waited nervously for the next instruction. As Big Ben stood up again, he jerked his head toward the defibrillator over his left shoulder. 'We have an injured man. He's close to death.' Shifting his eyes to Lord Hale, he said, 'It's Dr Parrish.'

Lord Hale glanced at the armed men to his left and right. Then he shrugged. 'I don't care. He is of no further use to me.'

The short man indicated with the barrel of his gun. 'Out. All of you. Where are the others?' We filed out, our hands held where they could see them, but none of us answered his question.

He didn't bother to ask twice. Instead, he jabbed his gun into Big Ben's ribs from behind. 'Think you're tough, do you?'

Now it was Big Ben's turn to shrug. 'Yes.'

It was a simple reply but not the one the short man wanted. He pulled his trigger to send a trio of shots into the wall behind us. Anne screamed, Lily screamed, I almost wet myself, but Big Ben just yawned. 'Put it down, tiny man and then we'll see how tough you are.'

'Boss,' one of the other armed men called to get attention. 'There's voices coming from this room.'

Now we were truly busted. The shots undoubtedly startled the rest of the dinner guests, and they had been heard.

With guns pointed at us, to make sure we didn't move, four of the six armed men readied themselves and kicked in the door. More screams and shouts of terror echoed out into the corridor, but we were all caught. Every last one of us.

The short man, who chose to personally lead the raid on Mary and Michael's room, now used a radio to call for reinforcements. They soon arrived, another half a dozen men, all wearing the same caterer's outfits and all armed with the same Heckler and Koch weapon. I worried they would just shoot Dr Parrish, but they let us take him, Big Ben and Professor Pope being pressed into the task of carrying his arms and legs.

'Where are you taking us?' asked Tempest's mum as they led us down the house's main stairs. I thought maybe she was stalling, or trying to get some kind of dialogue going, but she had other ideas. 'If you wish to lock us up somewhere, there's a perfectly good bar we were in before dinner. That would be ideal. Or you could put us somewhere else and bring the contents of the bar to us. That could work too.'

The short man spun around to face her halfway down the stairs. 'Hey, shut up, lady. We are not caterers, okay?

She kept her mouth shut. For about three seconds, which was just enough time for the short man to turn around and start walking again. 'Well, there's no need to be rude. You look like caterers. It even says Carter's Catering on your tunic.'

I saw the man twitch, his thumb hovering over the safety catch as he wrestled with whether to just shoot her or not.

We were led down the stairs and through a door and down some more stairs and then into an empty storeroom. Once inside, we all turned to look at our captors, hard stares being returned from all of them. Lord Hale hadn't come down with us, he stayed on the ground floor to supervise the rest of the house being stripped. It was clear that was the activity being undertaken. Oil paintings, statues, busts, all manner of objects were being carefully packaged and boxed. It was a slick operation though I still couldn't see the advantage for Lord Hale. What I was certain of was their need to eliminate any witnesses. I couldn't work out why they hadn't done it already.

So, when short man said, 'Don't worry, folks. We just need you out of the way until we are finished. No harm will come to you if you just stay here.' I didn't believe a word.

They were going to kill us, and the only reason I could come up with for stalling was that they wanted to make it look like an accident. How would they do that?

A Crazy Plan

The door to the storeroom shut with an ominous clang and the sound of an electronic keypad being operated. The noise of a solenoid clicking told me the door was locked, though I continued to stare at it until someone touched my arm. It was Tempest's dad, Michael.

'Are you alright?' he asked. The answer of course was yes, from a physical perspective. I had a number of bruises because tonight had been far more adventurous than expected and I was hungry and getting quite tired, but as I stifled a yawn, I had to admit that I was fine.

With a nod, I asked, 'How's Tempest?'

'Much better,' he said, appearing next to me. 'I have a corker of a headache, but the blurred vision has gone.'

'Just weak,' said Big Ben, throwing a casual insult for Tempest to ignore.

Tempest pulled me into a hug, more for his benefit I thought than for mine. To one side of the room, on the left if one was standing in the doors, lay Dr Parrish. Professor Pope was standing over him with a bag of plasma which

Lily already had going into a vein in his elbow. The professor was squeezing the bag to get the fluids in quicker while Lily administered a drug of some sort. They could prolong his downward spiral, stretch it out for a few more hours, but Lord Hale and his team gave the impression they were almost finished which had potentially terrible repercussions for all of us.

We needed to escape. It was a thought that was beginning to feel like a mantra, so many times it had echoed in my head this evening. I felt as if I had been fighting for survival for hours now, which technically I had. Always believing salvation was around the corner, always convinced we could get out and get away. Now we were trapped in a storeroom, our brief moment of freedom as we got out of the basement lasting no more than half an hour.

The storeroom's walls were painted white, the floor was concrete, and the ceiling looked to be as well. There were no windows. Big Ben was testing the door, seeing how solid it felt and looking for a weak spot when it refused to yield.

He stepped away and pulled a face. Then made like he was going to kick but changed his mind at the last moment. 'What do you think they kept in here?' he asked when he turned around to look at us watching him.

The storeroom was empty save for a few torn pieces of paper and some broken plastic banding. He was most likely right, and they had emptied the room earlier this evening, taking the contents as they had everything else of value.

'More artwork,' Michael hazarded. 'That seems to be what this is all about. Do you think it is insurance fraud?'

I had the same thought myself earlier, wondering if Lord Hale was clever enough that he could sell the artwork to black market buyers and collect the insurance money. I wasn't educated when it came to art, but during the course of my police career I attended a few burglaries where artwork had been taken. I was always stunned at the value associated with it.

Then a little itch tickled the inside of my skull. 'Michael, when the elevator opened and Lord Hale was waiting for us, did you notice how sweaty all the men were?'

He cast his eyes down as he pictured them. 'Yes, they were. Grimy and sweaty like they had been working really hard.'

'Did you notice that Lord Hale's dinner jacket was also grimy.'

He thought about it, slowly shaking his head when he reached an opinion. 'I can't say that I did. Was it?'

'Yes.'

Tempest looked at me. 'What've you got, Amanda?'

I puffed out my cheeks, trying to decide. 'Lord Hale looked like he had been working just like the other men. If they were getting dirty moving and shifting the artwork and statues and things, then their appearance makes sense. They were sweaty, but now when I picture Lord Hale's head, there was no sweat on his face. Their faces were grimy where they had got covered in dust moving old oil paintings and the sweat had tracked lines through it. His bore no trace of sweat but it was grimy. His hair was still perfectly in place too.'

'Okay,' said Patience, joining us as everyone else began to drift in our direction. There was nothing else for them to do. 'So, what is that telling you?'

'I don't think we were talking to Lord Hale.' I had said the same thing to Patience earlier, but then it was just a feeling. Now I was sure of it. My revelation was met with utter silence, which was better than everyone laughing at the suggestion. 'I don't think we have met him yet.' Now I got a few raised eyebrows. 'Think about it. He's grimy from lifting heavy boxes and crates as they take the art from this house and put it in their catering vans.' Everyone waited for me to make my point. 'He's supposed to be eighty years old.'

Everyone saw the incongruity at once. I berated myself for not seeing it earlier. Had I not been so preoccupied with Alexander the crazed murderer and poor Dr Parrish, perhaps I would have.

'He outran us.' The latest comment came from Big Ben. I had forgotten that. 'You said at the time that he must have taken a short cut to get to the stairs ahead of us, but he didn't, he just went faster. What eighty-year-old can do that?'

My mind was whirling now. 'Okay, so the Lord Hale we met this evening is an imposter. He is robbing the place, but Alexander turns up and starts killing the staff. His crew know nothing about it because it is all going on below the ground floor where they know they have us trapped, and he can't communicate with them because he wanted to make sure none of us could speak to the outside world. This place is bristling with electronics, but they want us to believe there is no mobile phone signal.' I stood on tip toes to look over heads to find Anne. 'Anne, you recognised someone when the elevator doors opened. Who were they?'

Anne, who was helping Lily with Dr Parrish, stood up and dusted off her hands on her dress. 'I knew them as David and Derek, though I suppose we have to question the validity of anything they said now. I met them weeks ago when Dr Parrish took me on, but they had been here much longer than that. They both work in the control room.' Their names weren't important, that they worked in the control room was because Lord Hale's imposter would need an inside man who knew how to work the system. Someone released the bats on cue. Someone controlled the knights. Now we knew who it was. Alexander must have killed Brian after he grabbed Derek from the dining room at the start of the evening.

There wasn't a lot of mystery to solve anymore. We knew who the bad guys were. We even had a pretty good guess about what they were up to. None of it mattered though because we were trapped inside a storeroom with an electronic lock on the outside and no way of escape.

The solenoid on the door made a popping noise and clicked.

All eyes turned toward it. They were back already. Their task was complete, and they had returned to dispose of us in whatever elaborate way they believed would throw the police off their trail. Well stuff that. I was going out fighting. Big Ben, Tempest, and his dad were already heading for the walls either side of the door. Frank saw them go and joined them, two each side. I wished I had a weapon of any kind as I crouched into a sprinting position. The second that door opened, I was going out of it, through whoever was first in line. We wouldn't get many of them, but maybe they only sent a small crew; three or four guys. If one of us managed to get hold of a weapon, we could turn the whole thing around and go hunting for the caterers.

The thought of that put steel in my veins. The door started to move. I started to run. The door was swinging open, and I was picking up speed. Big Ben and the others were all poised to swing around the doorframe once I barrelled through it and a face appeared in the widening gap to give me a target.

Too late, I realised the face I was just about to smash my way through belonged to Narcissus. I couldn't stop; I was right on her.

She screamed and tried to shut the door again, but I slammed into her, knocking her backward so she hit the wall opposite and then as I tried to apply the brakes, everyone else, led by Big Ben and Tempest piled through the door after me. No one else had seen who was there, they were just attacking like a maddened mob and hoping to live through it.

Shoved from behind, my cry of, 'Wait!' went unheard and I landed on top of the now crumpled Narcissus with bodies falling over and piling on top of us.

'Where'd they go?' shouted Big Ben, trying to get up. His face was right next to mine, his body squashing me quite convincingly.

The next minute was eaten up by everyone untangling themselves and working out which leg went with which person. With nothing to stop them, the surging crowd found free air and hadn't been able to stop, each person behind pushing the person in front until only Lily and Tempest's mum were left standing.

Mercifully, despite the crushing body slam I gave her, Narcissus was uninjured. A little shaken but conscious and able to walk. 'I saw the whole thing,' she said. 'They have cameras everywhere. I started to fiddle with them after you left, expecting to find they showed the escape room floors in the basement and maybe the dining room we were in, but they go all over the house. I could see them positioning themselves outside the elevator. I shouted at the screen, of course,' she admitted, her cheeks colouring. 'Is everyone okay?'

I wrapped her into a hug. She had just saved our lives. 'You risked a lot to come here alone to let us out.'

'Oh, err, no. It was nothing really.' She pushed away as I

let her go. 'I watched them all go back upstairs. There's no one on this floor but us.'

Big Ben stepped in to give her a hug as well, Patience slapping his arms down with an expression that dared him to try it again.

I was stunned to be free once more but there was even less time to lose now. 'How far to the control room from here?' I looked around as I asked.

'It's around the corner,' Narcissus said with a point. She wasn't lying either. It was less than ten yards from where they locked us up. They were sloppy. Lord Hale especially. If he had done a head count, he would have seen he was one witch short and then we would have been truly in trouble.

'What do we do now?' asked Gina.

I was standing in front of the console, staring at all the buttons and thinking about what the best scenario could be. When I spun around to face my fellow dinner guests, I saw a sea of expectant faces. They all wanted to go home, but I think they all knew we weren't getting out until we beat the bad guys. With a wry grin, I said, 'I have a crazy plan.'

Quinn

SUNDAY, DECEMBER 11TH 0454HRS

'Narcissus can operate the doors and windows from this console, and we can watch what is happening on these monitors. We have to do several things but none of them should put us in any danger.' I missed out that some of us were going to place ourselves directly in harm's way because I was selling them all a plan and most of them would indeed be tucked safety away from the bad men and their machine guns.

'First we need to lock them in wherever they are and disable the elevator.' With a smile, Narcissus took my cue and flicked a few switches. The screen flicked to show images on the ground floor including one shot which showed Lord Hale in the centre of the entrance lobby and the grand doors beyond. Another screen showed the elevator with two men in it. With some more switches flicked, a command typed into the keyboard, and a click of the mouse, the front doors swung closed. Then the windows we could see on the screens all went black as shutters outside folded in and then the elevator lunged to a stop, the

167

two men inside losing their footing to crash into one another.

'That's step one,' I announced, a happy bounce in my voice.

'What's step two?' asked Michael.

I pointed to the keyboard. 'Now that we have them off balance, we need to call for help.'

Patience frowned at me. 'The phones don't work, girl.'

I flipped my eyebrows at her. 'Try again.'

She gave me a questioning look, then said, 'It's in Mary's bedroom. They made us leave everything behind.'

Mine was dead. 'Anyone got a phone that works?' If no one did we could do it by email, but a phone would get a faster response.

It was Tempest who was first to hold one in the air. 'Sloppy of them not to confiscate them.'

I caught it as he threw it underarm in a lazy arc. 'I guess they figured we couldn't use them. Which we couldn't until Narcissus reconnected power to the mast.' I opened Tempest's contact list, scrolled through while trying not to note how great a percentage of the contacts were women's names and came to the one I wanted.

Waiting for it to be answered as it undoubtedly woke the person at the end, I pulled it away from my mouth so I could speak to Narcissus. 'Want to hit them with some special effects?'

Just as Narcissus was getting busy, the call was picked up at the other end. 'Chief Inspector Quinn.'

I took a moment to prepare myself. I disliked my former superior intensely. He was a stubborn misogynistic pig of a man, who rarely even looked down to see who he was step-ping on as he made his way to the top. He was, however, someone I could rely on to react. He would see the personal gain to be had and scramble all the forces he could muster. Telling myself I was ready, I said, 'Good morning, Ian, this is Amanda Harper, are you ready to make a huge bust?'

Next to me, Big Ben sniggered and echoed, 'Huge bust.'

I turned away so I wouldn't have to look at him using his hands to make the universal sign for big boobs and hoped Ian Quinn wasn't about to hang up on me. When he finally spoke, the bleariness was gone and the usual sneer I always heard when he spoke my name was back. 'Harper. I thought… No, make that prayed I had seen and heard the last of you. I will therefore assume that this is either a gloriously misguided attempt to waste my time, in which case I will be pressing charges, or, and I consider this far more likely, you have a genuine case for me. What is it?'

Behind me, Narcissus was using the voice changer to create the monster voice. 'I have come for you Lord Hale. I can see you and I know where you are. You have moments to live, Lord Hale, you and all your little friends with their puny guns. Nothing can stop me. I am a demon come to drag you all to hell.' She was really going for it, making her own voice as creepy as she could.

'Harper, I'm waiting,' prompted Chief Inspector Quinn. Letting the others have a little fun with some of the special effects, killing the lights and creating mist, I explained to the chief inspector where we were, what had happened and who he ought to send. In typical Ian Quinn fashion, he didn't bother to thank me, he merely growled, 'Don't tell me how to do my job, Harper. I'm far better at it than you.' Were it not for his self interest in making a big bust and solving a triple murder I thought he might have rolled over and gone back to sleep. As it was, he said, 'Stay safe and keep those civilians out of harm's way. The cavalry will be there soon.'

'Why don't we just let them escape?' asked Gina. 'If they are finished with the robbery, they can go, the police can catch them later and we can escape. Why do we need to bother with all this escape room nonsense? Isn't this just prolonging the time it takes to get Dr Parrish to hospital?'

Her questions were fair. I hadn't explained much to them yet. 'I don't think they plan to leave here with us alive.' That statement brought a few sharply drawn-in breaths. 'We have all seen their faces and they have pulled off a major robbery, taking hundreds of pieces of artwork which are probably worth millions. Think about it; they went to a lot of effort. Would they really leave a load of eyewitnesses behind?'

Professor Wiseman argued, 'Surely, if they were going to kill us, they would have done it already.'

Tempest answered him. 'That would make sense, but what if you had just emptied this place of all the artwork and wanted to ensure no one was looking for it. How would you make sure none of it was reported as stolen? Ever?' He let the question hang for a second before answering. 'I think they plan to burn this place to the ground. They can't shoot us because they need the police to find our bodies and determine that we died of smoke inhalation or just plain burnt to death.' There were more gasps.

Tempest's dad nodded. 'That makes perfect sense. We can't fight back because they are all armed and if they had to shoot one of us, they can just take the body and dispose of it elsewhere.'

'That's what I think,' I agreed. 'If we wait until they go, even with us sealing ourselves in here so they can't get to us, I think it likely they will still light the fires. The police will conclude we gathered here to hide, and the smoke or heat got us.'

'So we just trap them upstairs until the police come, yes?' Gina still had it wrong.

'If we do that, we expose the police to a fortified position filled with heavily armed criminals.' She put a hand to her mouth as she got what I was suggesting. 'We have to disarm them or otherwise separate them so they cannot form a coordinated response. Chief Inspector Quinn of the Kent Police is even now gathering his forces. He'll bring paramedics with him, but it will take an hour, if not more for them to get here and by then we need to have disarmed or effectively trapped all of Lord Hale's men. Otherwise, this might turn into a siege with us trapped inside. If that happens, it could be days before we get Dr Parrish to hospital.'

As my words sunk in, they could see the likely truth of them. None of us knew what the caterers had planned and anyone with a brain wouldn't want to wait to find out. Our only choice was to take the fight to them.

Now that they were on board, albeit, quite reluctantly in many cases, it was time to share out the tasks because most of us had a role to play.

Escape Room

The first task was one of the most dangerous, so it was no surprise when the three ex-servicemen volunteered. 'You're too old,' insisted Mary to her husband. She got a rude word in response.

Frank wanted to go with them, and no one was going to stop him, but then the remaining three men in the room, the three middle-aged and quite portly professors all felt they were failing to pull their weight so also volunteered. I didn't need any sexist nonsense in my life at any point, let alone now. Tempest, Big Ben, and Michael were handling this task because they had applicable training and were used to hitting people. The professors didn't need to be involved just because they were men.

Narcissus had stopped the elevator between floors just to make sure the two men inside couldn't go anywhere but flicked the power back on now. Professor Wiseman did his best to imitate Lord Hale's voice as he used the emergency speaker in the elevator to speak with them. 'Chaps, we got hit by lightning. It knocked out everything. We're just rebooting systems now. Won't keep you long but to be safe we're going to let you out at the next floor. You can make your way back from there.'

A husky voice replied, 'Just hurry, will you?'

'We're bringing you up now,' said Professor Wiseman.

'Just hurry up,' growled the first man again.

Big Ben thumped Tempest on the arm, 'Let's go, wet pants.'

I watched them on the monitor as the four men positioned themselves, two each side of the doors as they waited for the car to arrive.

In the elevator, visible on another screen, the two men I mentally named, Igg and Ook, were saying nothing and staring forward. My heart hammered in my chest as I counted down with the guys. Then the doors opened, Tempest and Big Ben threw themselves in and up, catching the muzzle end of the weapons to drive them upwards, thus ensuring any shots fired went in a safe direction. Igg and Ook then got a knee to the midriff apiece and were thrown out of the elevator as the two guys pulled their weapons away, turned and pivoted. Upon landing they found Frank and Michael weighing in to ensure they couldn't get up.

It lasted less than two seconds and not a shot got fired.

Not right away anyhow.

Narcissus offered me a fist to bump. 'Two down. Ten to go, plus Lord Hale.' It was a good batting average, but hardly a winning score yet. Rosemary and Hazel were on hand to help tie the caterers up, binding their hands and feet with yet more dream catcher string so the guys could drag them to the storeroom.

On their way past, Tempest stuck his head in the control room. 'Ready for the next bit?'

I nodded. 'Go for it.'

He raised a radio, freshly liberated from either Igg or Ook and pressed the send switch. 'Boss!' he yelled in a panicked voice. 'Boss, there's something down here.'

Lord Hale's voice came over the radio. 'Stop panicking and report, man.'

'Boss! Aaarghh! It's coming! It's…' then we heard a rip of gun fire as he loosed off a volley.

'Report, man.' Lord Hale waited for a report that would never come. 'Report!' he insisted. 'Heseltine, report.'

I figured that right about now his men were starting to get just a little creeped out. We could see it in their actions as we watched them on the monitors. Tempest wandered back in, making sure his weapon was set back to safe before letting it hang by the sling.

'Can this thing do a plague of toads?' asked his mum as she looked at the myriad switches.

'No,' grinned Narcissus, 'but it can do this.' Her hand hovered over a switch as she watched the screen in front of her face. Then, she hit it and all the lights went out in the entrance lobby. We heard a pitiful whimper of a scream and the lights came back on to show one less person visible. A man standing just a few feet from Lord Hale had vanished through the floor. In the darkened room, they didn't see what happened to him, but Narcissus had opened a trapdoor. It was supposed to send the person above down a chute like being on a playground slide, but Big Ben had *accidentally* disconnected it and moved it out of the way.

Big Ben returned a few moments later with the unconscious man hanging from his right hand like a child dragging a teddy. 'Did he hit his head?' asked Gina.

Big Ben smiled. 'No, sweetie. Big Ben hit his head. You should have seen it. I got him in midair.'

'Yes, yes, thank you, Ben.' I waved my arm to move him on. 'Please put him with the others.'

'Some fog?' asked Narcissus.

I nodded but I couldn't shift the feeling that we had been lucky so far. Six of the caterers plus Lord Hale were still in the main entrance lobby. They were trying to find a way out and I wasn't sure how long the house's defences would last. They were designed to deter celebrities from escaping, not a small military unit.

The main body of goons in the entrance lobby were forming up to start shooting out a set of windows. As thick fog started to seep into the room, we could see Lord Hale giving them verbal instructions, and though we had no sound with the picture, we could see when they opened fire and hear it echoing through the house.

Instantly on the radio, the nervous voice of another goon. 'What are you shooting at? Are you being attacked?'

'I think I saw something,' came another voice.

We could see who was speaking on our screens; the remaining nine caterers divided into three parties. Six in one, a pair, and a single. It was the pair who were the most jittery, so I chose to pick on them next. 'Can we force them down to the basement? Trap them in there?'

Narcissus poked a few buttons. 'I don't see why not.'

'What can we do to help?' asked Professor Wiseman, his beard grazing my arm as he leaned between me and Narcissus to see the screens.

I held up a finger to beg for a moment's grace and called Big Ben over. 'Ben, can you get back up to the rooms?'

'Is it time for a performance?' he asked. He looked neither keen to do it, nor desperate to avoid the task. It involved a definite degree of risk but might be key to winning. We discussed it earlier, when the first tendrils of a daft idea started to form in my head, and he had shrugged in usual Big Ben fashion; he was always up for anything.

'Dad,' Tempest called to get his father's attention. 'It's time to go.'

Mary asked, 'Why does he have to go?'

'Because it's in our room, love.' Michael gave his wife a hug and a kiss on her forehead. Then, the three guys ran out of the control room again.

Focusing on the screens again, I could see the main party had shot the window to pieces and were now examining their handiwork. All the glass was gone but the screens outside the window were still intact. Two men were trying to batter them open with the butts of their guns; they would get through eventually and then be able to escape.

On another screen, Tempest and the others appeared, getting into the elevator where they assumed the standard in-an-elevator position of eyes forward and stand still.

'Let's open a door, shall we?' I asked Narcissus, pointing to the pair of caterers separated away from the rest. They were on the ground floor, but I wanted them trapped below ground if I could achieve it. I was reducing the effectiveness of Lord Hale's party to repel an advance by the police armed response unit when they arrived. They were using up their ammunition, not that I knew how much they had to start with, and we were reducing their numbers. Trapping two in the basement, even with their weapons, meant they couldn't return fire on the police and were far more likely to surrender.

'I'll give them some motivation too. Watch this,' announced Narcissus with some glee. Patience, Gina and most others in the room crowded around the monitors. The door in the room they were in swung slowly open. The two men glanced at it, at each other and back at it. They pulled their weapons into a firing position. 'I'm giving them footsteps behind the wall.' As she said that and clicked the mouse, both their heads jerked around to stare at a wall behind them.

One of them lifted his radio and spoke into it. 'Guys, it's Eddie and Lou. We're near the dining room. Is anyone else back here? We can hear footsteps.'

Lord Hale lifted his radio. 'It's nothing you idiots. Ignore it. You all failed to secure the dinner guests properly and now they are in the control room playing tricks on us, just like Dave and Derek did to them.'

'It doesn't feel like a trick,' the nervous man replied.

'Ready?' asked Narcissus just so we were all watching. Another click of the mouse and the wall panel behind them changed to translucent and a gruesome creature that was half spider, half rat and one hundred percent the stuff of nightmares bared its teeth and lunged for them. Both men screamed and ran from the room.

We picked them up on another camera as Narcissus added hissing, screeching noises and controlled the doors to guide them toward the basements. They all but tumbled down the first set of stairs but, Narcissus added more mist from pumps embedded in the steps themselves.

Lord Hale was screaming for them to report, but they weren't listening. He changed strategy. 'Dave?'

'Yes, boss?'

'Where are you?'

'Trapped in the billiards room. I went back to check the fuses. Everything is set to go; this house will burn like a tinderbox when this goes. There'll be no trace left for them to work out what happened. All the police will find is dead dinner guests, one dead Lord Hale, and a mystery that will never be solved.'

'Yes. Except the dinner guests aren't where they are supposed to be and now have control of your control room. All the tricks you played on them earlier, they are now playing on us. Chances are they are listening in to this conversation.'

'You were right about the arson,' Patience whispered, unwilling to speak loudly in case we missed something the others were saying.

'Are you there, dinner guests?' asked Lord Hale. 'I shall assume you are. Well, you have tipped my hand, so we are coming for you now. No doubt the police will ask why the dinner party ended in a hail of bullets and where the guns came from but don't worry too much about that, I'll do my best to arrange you all so it looks like Alexander went nuts and you all killed each other fighting him.'

A stab of adrenalin hit my bloodstream causing me to glance up at the screen showing Eddie and Lou and their flight toward the sub-basement. They were below our level now and about to hit the last door, driven on by Narcissus and her special effects. I had just enough time to yell, 'Noooooo!'

I was too late to stop her from opening the last door. Eddie and Lou ran right at it, unaware of what might lurk on the other side just as Alexander threw the door open and burst out. The enormous man looked mad as all hell plus he had the advantage of surprise. The two caterers ran right into him; even though armed, their weapons were not ready to fire and neither man got up when Alexander hit them. Clubbing punches; one, two.

'Quick, shut the doors above him. Let's keep him trapped.' My alarmed instructions betraying my concern. I didn't want another player on the field, especially one so ready to kill.

Then all the lights went out to the accompaniment of several choked screams and gasps.

'Yes, dinner guests,' drawled Lord Hale's voice over the radio. 'I just operated the master switch. You didn't know about that, did you? Sorry. All your tricks just went away. None of the door locks work now, so get ready, because here we come.'

Final Stand

The lights came back on just as suddenly as they had gone off, the overhead lamps blinking and flickering as they settled. We had been in darkness so little time that no one had been able to fumble for a phone to create light to see by. The screens were coming back to life as well, Narcissus stabbing buttons and shaking the mouse to make it do something.

'Are we good?' I asked, pleading that we were. 'Are we back up?'

Her head was shaking impatiently as she tried to make the console work. 'It's rebooting. Probably it's rebooting from a server somewhere. This is going to be down for ten minutes or more.'

We didn't have ten minutes.

'What is working?' asked Patience, staring at the screens which were displaying pictures already.

Narcissus motioned with her head. 'The screens are, but I can't change which cameras feed them until the console comes back up.'

I turned to go. 'Then we need to get out of here. Everyone, grab your things and let's move.'

'What about Dr Parrish?' asked Lily. He was still unconscious, still a terrible colour and he wasn't going anywhere. My shoulder slumped in defeat; we couldn't leave him. It was the only sensible thing to do, but I wasn't going to do it.

'Patience and I will carry him. Everyone else, just get away from here. They will come from the left so go right and try to double around. The doors will be open now, so if you can make it to them, you can escape into the woods. The police are coming, but don't come back to the house until you are sure it is safe.'

No one moved.

'Go!' I shouted, grabbing Lily's arm and pushing her toward the door. 'We're right behind you!'

Jolted into action, the rest followed Gina and the professors through the door, terrified squeals and sounds of panic diminishing as they ran away.

'We're not going anywhere, are we?' said Patience. She knew we could carry Dr Parrish, but his weight would make us slow and ensure we were caught.

'You should go too,' I told her.

'Nuts to that, girl. This game isn't played out yet. Look at the screen.' She pointed with her eyes, and I saw it too: Lord Hale was coming, the short man at his shoulder and five more men behind him. The room that Dave had been in, the camera still pointing into it, was now empty, so he was heading in our direction too. What they didn't know was that Alexander was on a collision course with them, and he had a machine gun in each hand.

Leaving Dr Parrish, we both rushed back to the console to watch the screens. Lord Hale's men were making too much noise, assuming us to be unarmed, which we were not. Tempest had left one of the MP5s with me, so we had a chance to lessen the numbers if they got to us. I didn't think they would though, they were about to run into Alexander, and he had stopped walking to take up a fire position as he waited for them to round the corner ahead of him.

Because the screens were just monitors and produced no sound, it felt like I was watching an old movie. That was until the torturously loud sound of gunfire reached us through the control room door. We were all on the same level, the sound deafening for us so must have robbed those closest of their hearing. Between the cameras, we couldn't see everything, but we watched Alexander cut down three of Lord Hale's caterers in the first salvo.

The short man found a doorway that offered some protection so he could shoot back, as others tried to get back around the corner. Now there was a gun fight, and it was going to reduce the number against us even more. I was both jubilant and sickened as another one of Lord Hale's caterers tried to get back to safety only to get hit and sprawl across the floor.

Lord Hale had escaped, that much I could see, though I wasn't sure which way he had gone until he ran past a camera displaying its feed on one of the monitors. He was heading for the doors, and he was going to get away!

I slapped Patience on her shoulder. 'I'm going after him. If this thing comes back on,' I jabbed a finger at the console, 'help the guys. This isn't over yet.'

'Take the gun!' she yelled after me.

I was already running for the door. 'You keep it in case they get to the control room.'

I didn't like guns. I saw the need for them, but only because it was impossible to uninvent them. Others had them and were prepared to use them, therefore those who would protect the normal folk, had to have them too. I felt better leaving it with Patience though. The delay created by Alexander meant that Lord Hale's men might arrive late enough for the console to reboot. That being the case, their target would still be the control room.

I was going after Lord Hale, and he looked to be unarmed.

All the doors were still open, which meant I could run up the stairs to get back to the ground floor. I expected to have to find a circuitous route to get there in order to avoid the gun fight, but it had ended. Peering around a corner, the position Alexander had been in was now vastly devoid of a hulking killer, the corridor filled only with the groans and whimpers of the wounded.

I stepped around them, picking up guns as I went; no sense in leaving them armed, then raced through the house and up the stairs to the ground floor. As I came through the door at the top of the stairs, I heard a click, and it slammed closed behind me; the control room was live again.

'Wha-haa-haa!' the monster's voice echoed through the house.

Oh, lord, Patience was at the console.

'I'm gonna get you, tiny white man.' The monster now had racial motivation it seemed. It was almost embarrassing, but I ran on, across the central atrium which contained the sweeping double staircase and onwards toward the entrance lobby where I was sure Lord Hale had been heading.

As I came towards it, I saw him there, smashing his fists against the doors in frustration. They must have locked again just when he got to them. I wanted to get to him, however, between him and me, was Alexander, his killer's giant ham fists opening and closing as he stared at Lord Hale and relished the task ahead.

Mist started to seep in, filling the airspace around my feet to obscure them. Ahead of me Alexander began advancing toward his target.

A ghostly spectre appeared from the ceiling, swooping down toward Alexander with a terrifying screech. Patience was having a great time pressing all the buttons.

Lord Hale held up a hand to ward off his attacker. 'Alexander, I'm not who you think. You don't want to kill me.'

'Yes, I do,' Alexander replied calmly. 'I should have got the role. I was far better qualified to be the monster. I even believed the curse was true. I wanted to use the monster suit to kill you, just to make the legend live on. They took it from me though, those damned dinner guests, so I'll just have to wring your neck instead.'

The time for talk was over, Alexander closing the distance down the corridor with nowhere for Lord Hale to go. It shouldn't make any difference to me if Alexander killed Lord Hale, but I wanted them both in custody and once he was done with the man he wanted dead, would he then turn his attention on me?

As Alexander closed in, rescue for Lord Hale came in the most ironic form. Along the corridor that led to the large front doors, many rooms opened to the left and right. Lord Hale couldn't get to the first ones before Alexander so was affectively trapped, but just before the hulking killer got to the final pair of rooms, the monster stepped in front of him.

Alexander was so shocked by the gruesome creature's unexpected appearance that he threw himself backwards to get away. The large bear-like creature with its glowing eyes and spindly arms stared down impassively at the man on the floor. Then the killer chuckled. 'You gave me quite the fright. I know it's a suit though. I've been in it,' he bragged. 'Now step aside or I'll kill you first.'

'I don't think so,' said the monster in its awful razor blade on a chalkboard voice.

The standoff lasted half a second; just long enough for Alexander to make a decision and attack. The monster saw it coming, parried Alexander's leading arm away and kicked out his left knee with a foot coming left to right. As Alexander's weight buckled, a chop to his throat and elbow to his head put him back down on the floor. At which point, Patience operated the trap door he had come to rest on.

He made a girlish squeal of fright as gravity sucked him down, followed a second later by a heavy crashing noise at he hit the floor below; the chute was still out of place. I ran to stare through the hole to find Tempest and his father wrapping the semi-conscious killer up with parcel tape.

Were we done? Had we won? It seemed so unlikely that I found myself nervously waiting for the next surprise attack.

The monster loomed over me, reached up with both hands and pulled off its own head. 'That was fun,' said Big Ben, a goofy grin on his face as usual. Then, in an explosion of movement, he jabbed out an elbow to hit Lord Hale in the face. The old man had been trying to get to a discarded crowbar still lying on the floor from their art-stealing activities.

'Hey, Tempest,' I called down through the trap door hole.

'Yes, babe?'

'Got any of that parcel tape left?'

Pesky Kids

SUNDAY, DECEMBER 11TH 0622HRS

With Lord Hale's hands and feet bound, we set about the task of making sure we had accounted for all twelve bad guys and treated their wounds. Lily was working overtime, dressing bullet holes, a task made all the more difficult because Patience and I insisted their hands and feet be bound before she did anything.

Everyone chipped in. Well, almost everyone. When Gina and the professors asked how they could best help, I asked them to find their way to the tower. I had a hunch that was yet to play out. Mary hadn't asked how she could help, instead announcing that she was going to help everyone by finding refreshments. Ten minutes later, she returned carrying a heavy tray loaded with drinks from the bar.

We gathered near the entrance lobby, assembling the caterers while Patience made very sure to read each one of them their rights. It was her bust, twelve arrests in one night plus a major art theft, several murders and arson prevented.

186

The chief constable was going to love her; not even Chief Inspector Quinn could claim he had a hand in this one.

Alexander remained in the basement. He was just too heavy to carry back upstairs.

Our dinner party adventure had lasted all night, the first streaks of dawn beginning to light the world outside when the flashing lights of approaching police cars could be seen in the distance. They were still a mile off when we heard a knock at the front door.

We all looked at each other, curious expressions wondering who it could be. Tempest was nearest, swinging the door open and then laughing when he saw who was outside.

'It's not funny, Tempest,' snapped Jagjit. 'Alice and I have had a terrible night. The car broke down, we couldn't get a phone signal, we...' His voice tailed off as he stepped inside and saw the array of broken, battered, and beaten bodies, most of which were bound with tape like prisoners of war.

Alice came in after him, the newlyweds holding hands. 'Looks like we might have had it easy, sweetie.'

There was nothing any of us could do but laugh.

Two minutes later the police arrived. The first car contained Chief Inspector Quinn, who leapt out to lead the armed response unit as they slid to a gravel-slewing halt next to him. I let Patience go outside to meet them, hanging in the doorway to watch with many of the other dinner guests. She directed the paramedics to Dr Parrish, who was rushed out and away minutes later while Patience explained events to her chief inspector.

There was one important thing left to do; something I had been keeping in reserve for the right moment.

'They are all under arrest, yes?' confirmed Chief Inspector Quinn.

'Every one of them. I read them their rights myself,' confirmed Patience. She was getting appreciative looks from all the other cops.

'Then we should determine which need medical treatment and make sure that happens and take the uninjured directly to the station. This is Lord Hale?' he asked, pointing to the elderly man sitting on the floor.

'Yes, sir,' she replied.

'Actually, it's not.' All heads turned my way. 'This is.' I beckoned to my right where Gina and the professors were waiting just out of view. They came into sight with an elderly man on Gina's arm. He was upright and walking but had the gait and shuffling steps of a man in his twilight years. Just behind him was Travis, who they had also tucked away in the tower once he had escorted us to dinner.

Patience's head swung to look at him and then at the Lord Hale on the floor and then back at the new one. 'So, who's this?'

Sniggering to myself as another line from Scooby-Doo ran through my head, I said, 'Let's just take off the mask and see.' In two strides I had covered the distance to him, forcing Chief Inspector Quinn to take a step back. I reached behind his head and pushed my hands down inside his shirt collar until I found the edge. Then I pulled the whole mask off in one go.

'Ah, nuts,' said Patience. It was Matthew the hot porter she drooled over on our way in.

He looked really angry, but I couldn't help myself from begging him, 'Can you please say, "I would have gotten away with it, if it wasn't for you pesky kids"? Can you do that for me?' I was entertaining myself unnecessarily and getting odd looks from everyone else, but I didn't care. I was still riding on a high and surprised we had won.

I got to quiz Alexander as they were loading him into an ambulance and discovered that he had sent the doctored invitations. Unbeknownst to Tempest and his dad, Alexander broke his pelvis when he fell through the trap door. Not that any of us felt that bad about it, but they gave him morphine and it made him more pliable; I doubt he would have answered questions without the drugs. He had no idea that Matthew was up to anything; he actually thought they were friends but plotted to kill everyone during the first run through because he believed he could pin it on Brian. Brian's body would go missing, leaving the police to believe he killed Kevin and Lord Hale, Dr Parrish and others. The dinner guests would be witnesses to say they had seen the monster attacking people.

It was actually quite neat. His murderous revenge ruined Matthew's grand theft. His entire team was a unit of retired military personnel the police had been after for some time but couldn't be sure even existed because they left no trace. Ever. Just a few whispers and the faint hint of a clue every now and then.

The police found burn points all over the house: a toaster set to short out next to a pile of old newspapers; an unattended candle in a bedroom with a blanket next to it which would have helped the fire leap to a curtain. It went on. Matthew would have retrieved Lord Hale and Travis from the tower, put them downstairs with us and set the house to burn. Evidence gone. No one would look for traces of oil paintings in a pile of ashes.

I think we were all lucky to survive.

Miscount

An hour later, our wounds were dressed, we had on fresh clothes and our bags were packed. We were all glad to be leaving. Lord Hale had thanked us quite profusely for saving his life and his house and his future business.

The escape room / murder mystery thing had all been his idea. He was the one who hired Dr Parrish, a man whose knowledge of the macabre enabled them to devise all the wonderful tricks, special effects and gadgets. The story of the monster was real. The monster wasn't, of course, but it was a family legend where truth hadn't been allowed to get in the way of a good story. The library in the sub-basement was purpose-built for the enterprise but modelled on a real room in the house where one of his ancestors had indeed put much time and effort into researching the legend. Lord Hale had fudged a few facts, changed the dates when his ancestors died to make it look like they had all popped off on their eightieth birthdays and there you had it: a wonderful concept for an ultimate escape room.

He expected to make millions, though now he had a

number of setbacks to overcome, not least that most of his staff were dead. Lord Hale was seventy-nine and I couldn't help wondering, as he waved to us from the steps of his house, what might happen when his next birthday came around again.

We all left at the same time, the academics and the witches, Big Ben and Patience, who were travelling together surprisingly and probably heading back to his place, Jagjit and Alice, Tempest's parents and then he and I.

The long procession of cars peeled away and snaked back along the road from Hale Manor to civilisation. A yawn split my face, forcing my eyes closed as I put a hand over my mouth. I was exhausted but daylight and natural rhythms were keeping me awake. Tempest seemed okay but a concussion wasn't something to mess with, so he was going to get checked out today and I was driving in the meantime.

Following Big Ben's car, my mind on idle as I tried to stay awake, I felt a niggle at the back of my brain. 'Did we miss something?' I asked. I got no answer and looked across to find Tempest was already asleep. 'I missed something,' I said to myself, racking my brain to make it show me what it was.

Ahead of me, I saw the figure on Big Ben's back seat sit up to show itself. The short man was in the back of his car! That's what I missed. My sleep deprived brain looked for twelve people plus Alexander. It should have been the fake Lord Hale plus twelve plus Alexander. I had miscounted!

Big Ben's car swerved severely, careening across to the other lane and back again as his brake lights flared. I saw a flurry of arms and legs as a tussle broke out in the car. There was nothing I could do except watch.

The car stopped suddenly, the tyres locking up and I slammed on my brakes too.

The passenger door flew open, Patience's bum appearing as she backed out of the car dragging the short man with her. I could hear a flurry of expletives as she laid into him, punching him in his face and whacking on his arms when he finally got his hands up to protect himself.

Of course, protecting your face in front of Patience just means you have exposed something else. Patience appeared to get both of them with her knee, a huff of breath escaping the man as he sagged to the floor.

Dancing back to see if he had any more fight in him, Patience gave him a second, then looked across and gave me a thumbs up. A final kick pushed him out of her way so she could reach in to get some cuffs from her bag.

As Big Ben loaded the short man into the cargo compartment of his utility vehicle, Tempest let out a snort in his sleep. I put the car back into gear and pulled away again, promising myself that next week would be less insane than the weekend had been. Then I remembered the were-wolf case I had already started to investigate and sighed.

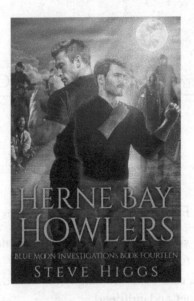

vinci-books.com/hernebayhowlers

Some people like to flirt with danger. These guys kick it in the balls and then shag its sister.

When two bikers are found half-eaten, the coroner's report records an animal attack. But England doesn't have any large predators … unless you count werewolves. Tempest Michaels is hired by the dead bikers' gang to find the truth. Everything points at their rivals, the Herne Bay Howlers. Their logo is a werewolf. But Tempest doesn't believe in the paranormal, and werewolves are up there on his list of fake nonsense he wants to kick in the nuts.

Turn the page for a free preview…

Herne Bay Howlers: Chapter One

KRAVEN SAYS

Friday, December 16th 1027hrs

I got the call yesterday morning, but it took me twenty-four hours to get to their house. The delay came about due to other work, a case I was working with Amanda Harper, my business partner and girlfriend.

My name is Tempest Michaels, I own and run a private investigation business which specialises in cases with a strange, unexplained, or paranormal element. You might think the number of cases available might be limited, but you would be wrong.

Very wrong.

Arriving in a career as a paranormal P.I. did not occur through choice, but as the result of poor luck. I have friends who call it fate or destiny though I believe in neither thing. It is true though that the success I enjoy through the paranormal speciality might not have been mine were my cases a little more ... vanilla.

I don't believe in the paranormal. Not one bit, so each

case is approached with the same expectation that an ordinary criminal, or someone with ill-conceived intent, is behind the strangeness I am called upon to investigate.

Today was no different. The call yesterday morning came from Harry Burke, a postman living in Cranbrook with his wife Agatha and fourteen-year-old daughter Paige. He was fraught with concern, his tone, like so many of my clients, bordering on desperate when he called me and begged for my help.

As I parked my car and let my two dachshunds plop out and onto the pavement, I thought again about the precarious line I walk with my trade. I know with unshakeable conviction that all my clients are deluded. They approach me to solve mysteries that have obvious answers, or crimes which have ordinary explanations. The Burkes' case would be no different. However, the issue is that I often feel like I am taking money under false pretences. I know they have fooled themselves into thinking something supernatural is happening when, in fact, it isn't and sometimes, they genuinely do need rescuing. Not from a poltergeist, or monster, but from a person who has chosen to target them. Rescuing people from a crime is rare though. More normally, I have to politely point out that they are stupid, and it made me feel bad when they then paid me.

'Come along, chaps,' I coaxed, and tugged their lead to guide them in the direction of Mr Burke's garden path. As I passed the car on their driveway, I noted the scratches and dents all along the side facing me. The paintwork was ruined, but not as the result of a crash or collision, someone had attacked it.

Mr Burke has been suffering a series of hard luck events, or so he originally thought. There were several small fires, including his garden shed which burnt to the ground with his tools, bicycle, and secret stash of naughty magazines inside. He also had a pipe burst inexplicably, the cat got shaved, and then there was the damage to his car.

He'd called the police, but there wasn't much for them to investigate. On the face of it, someone was playing tricks on him or waging an annoying hate campaign. Or so he first thought.

Unable to explain what was happening, he asked his daughter if she knew about it. Typically for a teenager, she denied all knowledge but then the couple awoke in the early hours of the next morning to find her standing at the foot of their bed with a kitchen knife.

They were a little freaked out.

The incident with the knife was last night and he called me at 0900hrs when business hours started because Paige claimed to be receiving messages that told her what to do. All the evil acts had been perpetrated by her, which meant Mr Burke no longer wanted the police involved. And he called me specifically because Paige said the messages came from hell.

As so often happened, the front door of their house swung open before I could get to it. Not in a spooky, the-house-knows-you're-coming-and-plans-to-eat-you-way, but because Mrs Burke had been watching for me from her living room window.

She looked to be fretting.

'Mrs Burke?' I asked, extending my hand.

'Thank you for coming so swiftly, Mr Michaels. I'm Agatha,' she sobbed as she took my hand. 'Paige is in her room and refusing to come out. She knows we hired you. Do you think she is possessed?'

Mr Burke appeared at the end of the hallway that led around their stairs. I noticed his right hand was bandaged and greeted him verbally without offering a handshake. The Burkes lived in a small semi-detached place on the outskirts of the small town. The carpets, décor, and general condition of the house, built probably circa 1930, was above average. However, in stark contrast to the couple's style the hallway wallpaper to my right bore a large crayon drawing of a severed head dripping blood. It hung from the hand of a beast with yellow eyes.

Mr Burke saw me looking at it as he approached. 'This is new,' he explained. 'We woke up to it this morning.' He put a comforting arm around his wife's shoulders.

'Is this Paige's work?' I sought to confirm. I had a good idea what was going on but no idea why.

They both nodded, Mr Burke sounding sad when he said, 'She's so emotionless about it all. She just says it isn't her and that she knows she is doing it but cannot stop herself or Kraven will get her when she sleeps.'

'Kraven?'

'That's what she calls it. Did I not mention that?'

With a shake of my head, I said, 'No. Do you know who or what Kraven is?' by my feet the dogs were fussing. I have two miniature dachshunds, Bull and Dozer. They are brothers, though not litter mates, and have been with me for several years. I take them most places I go, unless it is going to be dangerous or I feel it likely I will need to employ stealth – they don't do stealth.

'Kraven is the being who has invaded one of her toys. It's a pink bear plushy that she's had since birth,' Mrs Burke explained. 'It used to be called Mr Huggins and it's supposed to talk,' she added. 'But it used to say, "I love you, Paige," and, "A hug is like a warm blanket from your best friend," plus other saccharine phrases. It broke five years ago, but she refused to let us throw it out or buy her a new one. Now it talks to her again, but with a different voice.'

I felt my right eyebrow twitch involuntarily. 'You've heard it?'

'Oh, lord, yes,' Mrs Burke replied, her voice betraying a sense of fear. 'It was awful. It's like a monster inhabits that little bear. Its eyes glow a dark red like the pits of hell and when it talks, it knows who it is talking to. It said my name,' she croaked, still horrified by the experience.

'Mine too,' admitted Mr Burke. 'It said if I tried to separate Paige and Kraven I would choke to death on my tea. I haven't been able to drink a cup since.'

It wasn't what I expected to hear, but it changed my theory not one little bit. 'Can you show me the other damage?'

With a wordless nod, Mr Burke led me back through the house and into their garden. 'I take it you saw my car when you pulled up?' he asked as we walked.

'I glanced at it. When did the damage happen?'

'About a week ago,' he replied. 'It was one of the first *events*.' Whether deliberate or not, when he said the word 'events' he added a chilling tone to his voice. I noticed his wife shudder.

In the garden next door, their neighbour, a man in his fifties with pot belly and ill-fitting trousers, eyed them suspiciously.

'That's our neighbour, Mr Greys. His fish all died two nights ago. He says someone put bleach in his pond. We haven't asked Paige about that one yet, but I expect it was her.'

A charred pile in the corner, with several blackened shrubs around it, was the remains of the garden shed.

They'd called the fire brigade but by the time they could get water onto it, there was nothing left to save.

'Is that how you injured your hand?' I asked, inclining my head toward the bandaged digits.

He smiled ruefully. 'Sort of. I didn't burn it trying to save my belongings if that is what you are asking. I ran to turn on the garden hose.'

'There was superglue all over the tap,' his wife explained. 'He couldn't get his hand free and when he tried to yank it away, he left his palm stuck to the handle.'

I had to grimace at the mental image but also nod a salute of acknowledgement to the devious mind behind this spate of attacks. Set a fire and then booby trap the obvious garden tap – ingenious.

Sucking in a breath, I let it go slowly through my nose. The couple were looking at me expectantly. 'I think I ought to meet Paige.'

'She's in her room,' replied Mrs Burke. 'She won't come out and won't open the door.'

'Are you bothered if I force entry?'

Their eyes widened. 'Like break down the door?' Mr Burke asked, his voice almost a whisper as if we were talking about doing something illegal.

I frowned. 'Yes, Mr Burke. Most interior household doors are lightweight and very easily outwitted. They are also cheap, and likely to break before the frame which might require a carpenter to repair.' I was either going to kick the door in or go home. It was their choice.

Reluctantly, surprisingly so, in fact, they agreed that it was time to address the issue of the evil pink plushy bear toy. As we walked back to the house, I hit them with a few more questions: Had there been any trouble at school? Has she fallen out with her best friend or friends? Had they recently instigated any new rules?

I got it on the third attempt.

'Paige.' I knocked politely on her bedroom door. Thrash metal played on the other side at a volume one might expect of a deaf person or, since it was thrash metal, a person hoping to soon be dead. 'Paige, my name is Tempest Michaels. I'm a paranormal investigator here to deal with Kraven. Can you let me in please?'

Despite the deafening volume of the music, it increased in response to my question.

I knocked again and tried again and added that I would have to force entry if she didn't let me in.

'I think he means it sweetie,' shouted her mother in a soothing tone.

The response from Paige, verbal this time, was short, terse, and filled with the kind of language one might expect to hear in a dockworkers' bar.

I tested the door handle to make sure it wasn't open, then handed the dogs' lead to Mrs Burke. 'Could you hold the chaps for a moment, please?' I didn't wait for a reply. The moment her hand opened, her response automatic as I thrust the canvass strap in her direction, I swivelled from my left foot and drove out with my right. I wasn't wearing the right shoes for the job; leather oxford brogues because my army boots would not go with my casual outfit, but they did the trick, nevertheless.

My foot struck the door just beneath the lock, shattering the thin sheet particle board as it went right through. The impact jarred my leg, and I got a small splinter in my ankle, but the door exploded inward leaving the lock mechanism in place for a second. Then it fell to the carpet with a clunk.

A surprised squeal of alarm came from within the room

as the door slammed open but was cut off quickly as Paige remembered she was supposed to be in league with an evil toy. I strode into her bedroom with purpose, looked around for the device playing the music and yanked the power supply from it. Speakers might be wireless these days, but they still need electricity to work.

Immediately, the music switched to her phone which had been sending the music to her wireless device. In her pocket the noise came out tinny and quiet. I elected to ignore it, choosing instead to stare down at the moody-faced teenage girl.

'You have desecrated Kraven's sanctuary,' she growled in a deep voice. Paige Burke was really into the role she'd chosen. That was my first impression. She wore a pinafore dress and knee-high socks but the sock on her right leg had been allowed to slump down and it had several holes in it. Her face and hands were dirty, and her hair was a mess, hanging unkempt as if viciously backcombed. It partially covered her face where the girl employed makeup to make her eyes look sunken and dark.

I could understand how her appearance and behaviour were freaking her parents out. This was all new to them. For me it was just Friday.

'Is that Kraven?' I asked. From her left hand hung a pink bear. She held it by one paw, the smiley-faced animal dangling limply. 'I am here to commune with him.'

Nothing about her changed when I spoke. She didn't move; her eyes didn't even twitch. Until they did. A devilish smile parted her lips, and her eyes twitched to look at her mother. Mrs Burke, peering around the doorframe to see her daughter, gasped when her evil-looking child made eye contact. The parents were half the problem in my opinion.

Their reaction fuelled the girl's ridiculous act and made her want to do it all the more.

'Kraven will speak with you now,' Paige announced in a twisted sing-song voice.

I was about to speak myself when a dread voice emanated from the pink teddy. 'Who dares to desecrate my sanctuary?' the bear asked, its eyes flashing red each time it spoke. The voice was that of a man; a man with a very deep voice but hinting at the edges was a gravelly quality. As background to the voice were the sounds of beings in torment, wailing in the background as presumably they were tortured in hell.

Playing my part and trying to supress my smile as I dissected the voice, I replied, 'Tempest Michaels dares. I have come to cast you out, Kraven.'

Kraven the pink teddy bear laughed in response to my statement, a deep booming roar of belly laughs that went on a little too long. I waited patiently for them to end, casting my eyes around the room in a search for something very specific.

Still on the right side of forty, my experience of teenage girls' bedrooms was nevertheless a long way behind me, but I figured the habits of teenagers were relatively universal and timeless. I spotted what I was looking for hanging over the back of a computer chair. Feeling no need to be polite or ask permission, I invaded the young girl's privacy by picking up what I took to be her school backpack.

My actions drew the first emotional response from her, as she said, 'Hey! That's mine. You can't touch that!'

With a ziiiip noise, the backpack was open. Upending it over her bed spilled the contents.

Paige yelled, 'Kraven, he is messing with my stuff!'

Once again, the deep, demented voice echoed out from

the pink bear. 'You will suffer, Tempest Michaels. For your sins you will endure a plague of boils! Your life will be nothing but misery. Be gone from this place and leave my servant.'

'Why did you pick the name Kraven?' I asked conversationally as I picked through Paige's belongings. 'It's not a name I am familiar with. Is it from a game? I'm not much of a gamer myself. Or maybe you are better educated than I give you credit for and did some research to come up with the name,' I added, wondering if it came from a book. I could ask Frank, my local occult expert later. 'Either way, I think I'll use your real name … Kyle.'

I let the name hang in the air for a moment, waiting to see whether it would be the person inside the bear or Paige who spoke first.

It was neither.

'Who's Kyle?' asked Mrs Burke.

Paige's cheeks flushed.

I pressed onward. Speaking to Kraven, I said, 'Hey, I'm just guessing that it's Kyle doing the voice of Kraven because that's the name all over her schoolbooks with pretty hearts drawn around it. Paige for Kyle; that sort of thing.'

Kraven broke first. 'You said you were finished with Kyle.' It was still the booming deep voice but now it sounded whiney and upset, the demonic edge forgotten for a moment.

'What going on?' asked Mrs Burke.

I held up a finger to beg a moment's grace, then quicker than the pouty teenage girl could react, I snatched Kraven from her hand and tore its head off.

A phone dropped out, one of the cheap ones a person can buy for a tenner anywhere.

Paige screamed in horror. 'Mr Huggins!'

White fluff tumbled to the carpet as I dug inside the head to get to the LEDs someone had installed. Ignoring the angry teenager trying to retrieve the phone from my hand, I turned around to show her parents. 'Someone took Mr Huggins apart and gave him some upgrades.'

There were tears running down Paige's face, but she was going on the offensive, rounding on her parents as they stared at her in disbelief. 'This is all your fault! You drove me to do this.'

'H – hello?' said Kraven.

I still had the phone in my hand. Lifting it to my face, I considered what I wanted to say. 'Would you like to give me your real name?'

After a beat of silence, which was only silence at his end; at my end it was bedlam as the angst-ridden teenager railed at her parents for cruel and unnecessary behaviour, Kraven said, 'Um, no. I don't think I should do that.'

I drew in a breath. I could just about remember being a horny teenage boy and getting suckered into doing things because a girl asked me to. Despite my feelings of empathy, the Burkes hired me to expose the truth behind their mystery, so I pressed on. 'Young man, I'm afraid I'm going to have to insist. And here's the reason you should. If you don't, I'll just come and find you. How hard will it be for me? You'll be the one in her class looking guilty tomorrow when I turn up at the school. Would you rather avoid meeting me?'

'Daniel,' he blurted. 'It's Daniel Bennett. I didn't know she was going to start setting fires. She said she'd go to the Christmas dance with me if I helped her.'

Barely able to hear him with the ruckus going on four feet from me, I gave him a few words of advice, let him know he was being used and ended the call.

Paige was most certainly not the first teenage girl ever to revolt against her parents' strictures. When I asked earlier about trouble at school or any new rules, they told me she had a new boyfriend and wanted to be out later than they would allow. I didn't ask the name, I didn't need that information, and I knew all about it now because the tear-soaked girl was screaming her displeasure at the top of her lungs.

She ignored their instructions, came home after midnight and they stopped her going out the next day. That was more than a month ago, the young man, Kyle, was older and had less strict parents, I guess, but he dumped her to date a girl who could stay out late. Or had bigger boobs perhaps; young love was a fickle thing.

Whatever the case, I felt certain of two things: 1. Kraven was gone for good. 2. Paige was grounded until she turned thirty.

It took a few moments to get someone's attention because I was attempting to be polite. When finally, Mr and Mrs Burke stopped shouting at their daughter, I said, 'I believe we can close the case, yes?'

Mrs Burke had a vein visibly throbbing next to her temple and Mr Burke was red in the face, possibly from counting the cost to repair the damage wrought by his daughter.

'How did you know it was a boy's voice coming from Mr Huggins?' he asked.

I tilted my head in question and frowned when I asked a question in return, 'What made you think your daughter possessed an evil toy?' It was a rhetorical question; I didn't want to hear the answer. I met people every day who, for whatever reason, have convinced themselves a non-rational explanation is the one that fits. 'Did you notice that Kraven had a local accent?' I asked before he could attempt to answer.

His mouth opened and closed like a fish. 'No, I didn't notice that.'

I flipped my eyebrows and shot my cuff to check my watch: 1053hrs. 'I'll let myself out. My accountant will send over a final invoice before the end of the week.' Or I would probably do it myself, I thought, because the person who had been doing the accountancy work was now solving cases instead.

I collected Bull and Dozer from Mrs Burke. I'd thought they might come in handy; that was why I'd taken them with me and all the way up to her room. Cute sausage dogs who roll pathetically onto their backs at the first sign of any attention coming their way, are always a hit regardless of age, gender, or sexual orientation. Had I needed to win Paige over, they might have proved useful.

In the end, they were unnecessary, but I liked to take them places with me; it meant I never had to wonder where they were or if they were alright.

'Case solved before lunch,' I commented as I made my way back to the car. 'I think that calls for a treat, dogs. Don't you agree?'

I got no answer, of course, but vowed to stop off for some treats to put in the office. It wasn't something I did very often, but I felt buoyant and positive this morning. Little did I know the drama awaiting me.

Herne Bay Howlers: Chapter Two

WOLF ATTACK

Friday, December 16th 1147hrs

My office sits toward the bridge end of Rochester High Street where it has an enviable amount of trade walking by it. I augment that by advertising in local magazines and newspapers with the combination delivering enough business to keep three detectives busy. Mostly we work our own cases, though sometimes it is necessary to draw in one or more of us to focus on a singular investigation. There can be many reasons for this but the usual two are that it looks likely to result in a violent altercation or there is a high bounty for reaching a solution.

We actively avoid the former and constantly seek the latter.

Rochester High Street is a wondrous place with quaint little shops which have stood for centuries. The businesses inside them may have changed many times over the years, but a few boasted signs to say established in 17somethingor other. One or two were even earlier than that.

Mr. Morello's Royal Cake Shoppe was at the Chatham end of Rochester High Street where it was sandwiched between a butcher's shop and a pub. The row of buildings was a later addition to the buildings nearer to the castle and cathedral which sat at opposite ends of the long, straight, cobbled road, but they were still more than two hundred years old.

I hadn't been in the confectioner's shop for years; sweet treats just didn't have a place in my diet. Telling myself I could relax for a day, I strode in to inspect their cabinet of cakes. Two minutes later, with my wallet twenty pounds lighter, I left the shop holding a box of filled donuts. They were expensive, but also hand-crafted and unique: If one is going to buy a treat, one should indulge.

The box was getting a lot of attention from the dachs-hunds who could smell the sugar inside. I'd parked the car behind the office in my usual spot – the office had three reserved parking spaces – and walked along the High Street to the cake shop. This close to Christmas, the picturesque central business area of the town was filled with the smells of street sellers hawking bags of hot chestnuts or roast pork sandwiches. I counted no fewer than five mulled wine outlets, and the mile-long street had been decorated elegantly to reflect the traditions of the season.

Walking back through it and soaking in the sights and sounds made me smile. I felt warm inside, buoyed by my relationship with Amanda and aware that, due to my flour-ishing business, I had no financial worries which meant I rarely worried about anything. The beautiful blonde woman who chose to lavish me with her affections did, however, present one minor hurdle – what to buy her for Christmas.

We were spending it together at my house. My parents were travelling to my sister's place in Hampshire on

Christmas Eve where there were grandchildren to enjoy. My mother was kind enough to accentuate her reason for going in front of Amanda as if the mere mention of grandchildren would make her ovulate. Amanda's mother was on a cruise around the world so neither of us had people we needed to be with. I was invited to also join my sister and her husband at their house; it would be a big family feast, but a quick discussion regarding Amanda's plans led to our decision to spend it together. Honestly, it was a lot more enticing than being Uncle Tempest the ride-on horse for the day.

She and I had only been dating for a few weeks, but I was smitten; I could admit that to myself, but it took me back to the question of what would make an appropriate gift at this time of year? I passed jewellers and a lingerie shop, a florist, and a confectioner selling imported pralines from Belgium. Items from any or all of these might be appropriate, but what would be considered over the top and what might make me look cheap?

It made my head hurt.

My musings took me all the way back to the office, where I shouldered my way through the front door with thoughts of hot, dark coffee on my mind.

I walked into a stand-off.

There were two men in their late thirties ten feet in front of me. Each was broad shouldered with scruffy, short hair. However, the standout feature was their matching leather jackets with matching motifs. They were part of a biker gang, which didn't make them bad people. Their actions, however, did.

They had their backs to me and were faced by both Amanda and Jane, who looked nervous enough to put me on immediate high alert. I needed less than a second to assess the situation and only the rest of the same second to reach a decision.

I dropped the dogs' lead, threw the box of donuts onto the reception counter, and as my actions drew their attention, I stepped into their personal space.

I didn't want a fight inside my office, but it wouldn't be the first time I didn't get what I wanted. I was going to have one shot at defusing whatever situation I'd walked into. After that, these men were leaving by force.

'Good morning, gentlemen. What seems to be the problem?' The words came out through teeth that were very nearly clenched as I did my best to make my posture seem relaxed.

Amanda answered, 'They wish to hire you, Tempest.'

I narrowed my eyes, never taking them from the two men's faces. 'Is that a problem?'

'Apparently so,' growled the man to my left. He had a three-day stubble and a thin line of scar tissue running along the left side of his face from his chin to his ear. 'According to miss Sugar Tits here,' I didn't need to see Amanda's face to know that she just cracked her knuckles at his comment, 'we are known criminals.'

'Yeah,' said his partner. 'Neither Bear, nor I have ever been convicted of a crime. She besmirches our good character.' He managed to sound forthright and wounded though I barely noticed it because I was still wondering about his name.

'Indeed,' complained Bear. 'We find ourselves eternally stereotyped because of our clothing choices and preferred mode of transport.'

Amanda snapped, 'I arrested you twice myself, Bear Knox. Once for possession of a firearm. You only got off because you had a good lawyer and the weapon had been wiped clean of your fingerprints.'

'That's slander!' he protested. 'You have no proof my fingerprints were ever on it.'

'A fine example of the discrimination we suffer daily at the hand of bigots,' added Bear's colleague.

Amanda's eyes flared but he had her; there could be no proof his fingerprints were ever on the weapon. They were not being overtly threatening, so I pushed forward, hoping we could soon wrap this up and get them out of our office.

'Then tell me, gentlemen, what is it I can do for you today?'

They glanced inward toward each other in confusion as if I ought to already know the answer to my own question. 'We wish to hire you?' said Bear.

Oh, yes. Amanda already told me that.

I invited them to join me in my private office at the rear of the building. There were two of them, one each for Amanda and me, though we were now working out how to share two between three detectives. If Jane was going to take on cases of her own, then she deserved equal treatment.

Closing the door defused the situation between the men and my ex-police girlfriend, Amanda. I would get a full blow-by-blow account from her later, but for now, it felt right to indulge their request, listen to their story, and then kick them to the kerb.

The two men were called Bear Knox and Ellis Jarrett, though their club names; the ones they wished to be known by, were Bear and Elk. I got the impression all the club members would have animal names like it was the boy scouts or something. They matched each other in height, haircut, facial hair, and clothing. Beneath their faded brown leather jackets, each wore a grubby white t-shirt, dark denim jeans and black leather boots of a style I thought of as biker boots. They were both full members of the Whitstable Riders' Motorcycle Club.

When I asked what they did for a living, Elk said, 'Various entrepreneurial enterprises.' It was deliberately vague and supported Amanda's claim that they were criminals.

I repeated my question from earlier, 'What can I do for you, gentlemen?'

'We need to hire you,' said Bear for the third time.

'More specifically,' I begged. 'I assume you have a case for me to investigate.'

Elk shifted in his chair, the leather of his jacket squeaking against the leather of the chair in the quiet of my office. It was Bear who replied. 'Two of our club members were murdered,' he announced.

Murder in Kent is rare enough that it tends to make the news, yet I'd heard nothing about two men being killed.

Seeing my frown, Elk added. 'Their deaths were listed as animal attacks. That's why you haven't heard about it.'

His comment connected the dots in my head. There had been a small article in the local newspaper last week. Two men were found partially eaten in woodland close to the coastal town of Whitstable. I couldn't recall anything else about it.

'So, you want me to find out what happened to them?' I enquired. 'You believe they were murdered?'

Both men stared at me, their eyes hard. 'We know they were murdered,' said Elk.

'And we know who did it,' supplied Bear.

'But we have no evidence,' cut in Elk again.

'And we want you to find it,' finished Bear.

I met their eyes as I considered their claim. It caused several questions. I led with, 'Tell me who did it.'

'The Herne Bay Howlers.'

The answer came from Elk, the men taking it in turns to speak as if it had been agreed in advance. I didn't know who the Herne Bay Howlers were but guessed correctly that it was a rival biker gang.

'Motorcycle club,' Bear corrected me. 'We are not a gang. The term gang is synonymous with illegal activity and carries unwarranted negative connotations.'

I had to admit the two men spoke more eloquently than I expected: their range of vocabulary far beyond the average person. It meant they were educated, but that, if they were engaged in criminal activity, just made them more dangerous.'

'This sounds like a case for the police,' I stated to see how they would react. Had they avoided the police because they didn't want the authorities looking at their activities?

Elk nodded. 'As we already expressed, Mr Michaels, the coroner recorded the deaths as animal attacks. The police have nothing to investigate.'

It was a fair point. 'What makes you think they were murdered?'

Bear leaned forward to get his face closer to mine. 'We know they were murdered. The Herne Bay Howlers have been taunting us. They are using terror tactics to scare our members into leaving and our president believes they are trying to move into our turf to take over our operations.

'What operations?' I pressed them again.

'Various entrepreneurial enterprises,' Elk repeated, his voice emotionless. I would have to find out for myself if I chose to take their case. I still couldn't see where I came in.

Finally, Bear stopped beating around the bush and

explained why they chose to single me out for their case. 'The Howlers are werewolves, Mr Michaels, and the animal attacks are exactly that. We have seen them in their transformed state.'

As was their habit, Elk took over. 'Our ability to defend ourselves against werewolves is limited. We are currently seeking a supply of silver bullets, but we cannot predict where and when they might attack.'

'At night seems obvious,' added Bear. 'However, we do not know how much of our supposed knowledge about werewolves comes from fiction and how much is accurate. That is why we approach you today. Will you help us, Mr Michaels?'

'We may be a little rough around the edges, but the men who were killed were our friends. We want justice for them, and security for ourselves.' His final point delivered, Elk sat back into his chair. Both men watched me to see what I might say.

On the face of it, this case was right up my alley. A gang of bikers posing as werewolves to augment the fear factor as they attempt a hostile takeover? Just my cup of tea. Maybe they did murder the two men, it felt plausible, but why then would the coroner state it was an animal attack? I would have to look into it. Bear and Elk were asking me to investigate a double homicide and offering to pay me for it. Why would I want to say no? In my head, the answer floated back instantly: because they are most likely criminals and their various entrepreneurial enterprises could be anything from drug smuggling to prostitution and everything in between.

Should I take the case or not? That was the question.

As the silence stretched on, I rapped my knuckles on the desk and made a snap decision. 'Ok, chaps. I'm willing to perform a preliminary investigation.' I met their eyes, first Elk and then Bear. 'I want you to know that I will not associate myself with criminal activity. If I get the sense that your ... enterprises,' I used their word, 'might cause my business embarrassment, I will walk away. Is that understood? If I see anything I don't like, I'll bail.'

'Understood,' said Elk.

That appeared to be all they had to say on the subject. I let go of a breath I didn't know I was holding and pushed back my chair. 'We need to discuss fees.' I was going to walk them through my usual explanation of charges and expenses but with an additional tariff added on because I still wasn't entirely convinced taking the case was a good idea.

Before I could get into it, Bear took a fat white envelope from the inside pocket of his leather jacket. 'This should get you started,' he said, placing the envelope on the desk. 'That's ten grand.'

I looked at the envelope. That much cash suggested they operated a cash business, doing deals under the table and claiming none of it to the tax man. There was nothing illegal about me taking their money, provided I filed my tax assessment correctly. That did not, however, make it all above board. I was making assumptions about them that were yet to be proven true. They complained that the world possessed and employed a bigoted view of them; refusing to take their money would be the same thing. I picked it up. 'I'll get you a receipt.'

Grab your copy...
vinci-books.com/hernebayhowlers

About the Author

When Steve Higgs wrote his debut novel, *Paranormal Nonsense*, he was a captain in the British Army. He would like to pretend that he had one of those careers that must be blacked out and generally denied by the government, and that he has to change his name and move constantly because he is still on the watch list in several countries. In truth, though, he started out as a mechanic - not like Jason Statham in the film by that name, sneaking around as a hitman, but more like one of those sleazy guys who charges a fortune and keeps your car for a week even though the only thing you went in for was a squeaky door hinge.

At school, he was largely disinterested in all subjects except creative writing, for which he won his first prize at the age of ten. However, calling it the first prize he won suggests that there were other prizes, which is not the case. Awards may yet come, but in the meantime, he enjoys writing mystery and thriller novels and claims to have more than a hundred books forming a restless queue in his mind because they are desperate to be written.

Now retired from the military, he lives in southeast England with a duo of lazy sausage dogs. Surrounded by rolling hills, brooding castles, and vineyards, he doubts he'll ever leave, the beer is just too good.